She'd thought she was safe, thought they couldn't find her—but she'd been wrong…

She heard James close the back door behind him and stared at the ceiling for a while, enjoying the moment until deciding to go ahead and make some coffee. She sat up and stretched a long moment before pulling on her jeans and top and walking lazily to the kitchen. She found a bag of coffee grounds in the refrigerator, filled the pot with water, and set it.

She was standing with her arms crossed when she heard the back door open again, a little more slowly this time. Knowing that James couldn't have been to the store and back by now, she called, "You forget something?" without looking back.

A large arm grabbed her then and, before she could react, a cloth covered her mouth. She remembered breathing in to scream, but then she became instantly drowsier than she'd ever been. Her head fell onto a foreign shoulder and, before she could get scared, everything turned to black.

Two days before Christmas, shy bookstore owner Scotlyn Carter survived a traumatic bank robbery and subsequent kidnapping. Now, three months later, she still wakes up hearing the robber's promise to find her—and kill her.

Then James McIntyre, the high school flame whose easy smile and mysterious eyes she could never forget, walks back into her life. As she falls for him once again, Scotlyn slowly begins to feel safe for the first time in a long time and thinks that maybe her nightmare will not come true, after all.

But James is not all that he seems. He is back in Scotlyn's life for a reason and has been in contact with the very thieves who kidnapped her. And he's harboring a dark secret that, if brought to light, could not only destroy their relationship—it could end their very lives.

KUDOS for *The Good Thief*

In *The Good Thief* by Tanya W. Newman, Scotlyn Carter is kidnapped by bank robbers, one of whom believes she has seen his face. She manages to escape, but lives in fear, knowing the bank robbers are looking for her and, if they find her, they will kill her. Just as she starts to relax, her old high school boyfriend comes in to the bookstore where she works with her father. Scotlyn hasn't seen James in years, not since he left abruptly after walking her home from school. But she has never forgotten him and hopes they can now take up where they left off in high school. But James is not what he seems, and he has sought Scotlyn out for a reason. Just when she thinks she can trust again, she learns that everyone has secrets. This is a well-written romantic suspense, with interesting characters, a strong plot, and plenty of tension. You just can't help rooting for Scotlyn and hoping that James doesn't turn out to be a scumbag. A good book for a rainy afternoon and a hot cup of tea. ~ *Taylor Jones, Reviewer*

The Good Thief by Tanya W. Newman is a story of young love, revenge, betrayal, and greed. Our heroine, Scotlyn Carter, is just getting over being a hostage in a bank robbery when an old flame from high school, James McIntyre, waltzes back into her life. Scotlyn had a major crush on him in high school and, just when she thought they might have something together, James disappears, moving away from their hometown. Now he's back and he's a hunk. And Scotlyn falls fast and hard. But James isn't all he seems to be, and there isn't room in his life for an old, or new, love. At least that's what he tells himself. Even worse, he's afraid he may get Scotlyn killed. And that's when the trouble really starts. The Good Thief is a solid romantic suspense, with a complicated and interesting plot, intriguing characters, and plenty of surprises to keep you on your toes. A great read. ~ *Regan Murphy, Reviewer*

ACKNOWLEDGEMENTS

My path to becoming a writer and writing *The Good Thief* would not be complete without the help, love, and encouragement of so many people throughout the years of my life. I would like to send a huge thank you to the following, beginning with the earliest and ending with the most recent in this journey:

God, for granting me the inspiration and love of writing.

Papa, for reading and loving my first book and for everlasting encouragement.

My mom, for being my best friend and for always believing in me.

My dad, for the many bookstore trips and for showing me that writing is in my roots.

My husband, Mark, for patience when I write and for sharing my love of a good story.

Dr. Marilyn Knight, for reigniting my love of writing and inspiring me to major in English.

Keith Lee Morris, for wisdom and encouragement that helped me continue to grow as a writer.

Barbara Culbertson, for being my honest and loving reader; your radiance will last forever.

Connor and Lydia, for showing me the meaning of life and love.

Lauri Wellington, for offering me a contract and a chance for my dream to come true.

Reyana and Faith, for their outstanding editing and for making this book better.

The

Good

Thief

TANYA NEWMAN

A Black Opal Books Publication

GENRE: ROMANTIC THRILLER/ROMANTIC SUSPENSE

THE GOOD THIEF
Copyright © 2016 by Tanya Newman
Cover Design by Mark Newman
All cover art copyright © 2016
All Rights Reserved
Print ISBN: 978-1-626944-42-8

First Publication: APRIL 2016

Published by Black Opal Books **http://www.blackopalbooks.com**

I dedicate this book to Connor and Lydia,
my two little gifts from Heaven.
Your smiles, enthusiasm, and love are the
brightest spots in every one of my days.
I love you both to the moon and back!

Chapter 1

*S*he could feel the end of the shotgun moving her hair over her ear and the tears silently creeping out of her tightly-shut eyes. She was shaking against the cold, wet leaves on the ground. Her breath was ragged with what little air she could take in.

Please, *she thought.*

The man holding the shotgun only stared down at her.

"Please, what? What did you see?" he demanded in that severe, brusque voice she'd become all too familiar with, able to read her thoughts, as always, before pulling the trigger...

☙❧☙

Scotlyn Carter opened her eyes to the darkness. She couldn't see anything before her, only blackness. She touched her hand to her face, feeling, as she knew she would, the wetness from the tears that always emerged from the dream into reality. She closed her eyes against the darkness, waited for her heart to slow, and forced herself to take slow breaths as she pushed herself toward consciousness and the reminder that it was only the same dream, the same nightmare. At least she was now able to sleep with her back to the door, in her own house. For a month after the robbery and subsequent kidnapping, she'd camped out on her dad's sofa.

Scotlyn turned over in bed now, looked at the clock's red digital numbers, and saw that it was a little after seven. She'd slept all of six hours.

Not bad, she thought. Sleep and relaxation had been a memory, stretching back three months to late December, the twenty-third to be exact. Scotlyn had a feeling she'd always remember that date and even fear it…

☙❧☙

She'd just finished making the store's deposit for the day and had turned to make her way out of the bank. Three men, large in stature and voice, wearing long black coats and black hockey masks, and carrying shotguns had burst in and ordered everyone on the floor, except the poor teller, who Scotlyn had been judging as wearing too much makeup and hairspray for a woman obviously in her fifties. Everyone started screaming, throwing their hands up, except for Scotlyn, who'd immediately hit the floor as if she'd been through this numerous times and knew the drill by heart. She'd never been much of a screamer, never been much of a talker, anyway, so she really didn't feel surprised at her reaction. They'd ordered the teller to give them all of the money in the bank drawer before shoving her back to the vault and clearing most of that, too.

All Scotlyn could think about in those moments as she pressed her face to the cold linoleum floor was, *This is really happening. These men are going to kill all of us.*

But they didn't. They were fast, professionals at what they did, obviously, and were out in probably less than two minutes, though one had made a simple, costly, mistake. Scotlyn had turned her face to the side, watching their booted feet move back and forth, not really knowing what was happening exactly, until she heard one of the men curse.

Against the voice screaming in her head, she turned her eyes toward the voice and caught a glimpse of his profile, only for a split second as he secured his mask once again. She'd shut her eyes tight as she saw him turning toward her and fought with everything inside of her not to scream as he walked slowly over to her. She could feel the end of the shotgun moving her hair over her ear and the tears silently creeping out of her eyes. The man never said a thing, only stared down at her, or so she guessed, until another man's voice said, "*Let's go!*"

That's when he spoke, when he said the words that would forever resonate with her. "She *saw* me, man! Saw my face! I've got to shoot her!"

"No!" Scotlyn had screamed, feeling the sobs shake her body as the end of the shotgun moved over her hair. "I didn't see anything, I swear!"

She would have said anything to keep that gun from going off.

One of the bank robbers, apparently the leader of the trio, came and stood by this one. "Are you sure? Are you *absolutely* sure?"

"Hundred percent."

"No," she reiterated, shaking her head.

"Clock's ticking," the robber near the front warned.

Scotlyn could feel the hesitation in the leader, then heard him curse before saying, "Put her in the van."

"What?" the one she'd seen shrieked. "I can just shoot her now."

"No!" the leader commanded. "Not here, not now."

"But—"

"Just get her and come on!"

He hauled her to her feet, turned her around, and fastened a bandana, tight, over her eyes, seemingly all in one movement. She couldn't see a thing, and it hurt, too.

"No," Scotlyn said again as he grabbed her and threw her over his shoulder, sack of potatoes style. "Please!"

Wow, he's strong, she couldn't help thinking. She didn't weigh much, but still, the way he was able to just throw her over his shoulder with one arm like that.

"Shut up!" came his answer to her plea. "We're going for a little ride."

Oh no, she'd thought. *This is going to be bad, so bad.* She was never going to see her father, or her best friend, Jane, ever again. And they were probably going to read or see on the news about her dying in a ditch somewhere.

They made it outside, and Scotlyn could feel the crisp air surround her just before he flung her into a van and climbed in after her. Things were getting real.

"*Go, go, go!*" he screamed before he even got the van door closed and the driver sped the vehicle into motion. She could feel him swerve right.

Down South Harper Street, she thought as the sharp turn shoved her against the door to her left. She could feel the door handle, could feel the cold air from outside, and could make out that the door was slightly open, had probably been left ajar without them knowing.

And that's when a plan started forming in her mind. But could she make it happen? Would she be able to do it?

"We taking her back to the house to do it, man?" the man beside her asked.

It she repeated, knowing exactly what he meant.

"Shut up! I can't believe how stupid you were!" the driver said, and they started bickering back and forth about stupidity, ignoring her.

Dead at their hands, or a chance to live on the road, she thought, and, realizing her choice, grabbed the handle, pulled as hard as she could, and threw her blind body onto the road without another thought.

She hit the ground hard, much harder than she would've thought, and rolled several times. She didn't see or hear any other cars and thought about how that was good, and bad, at the same time. She'd barely stopped rolling when she got up, yanked the bandana away, and started running.

Her head was spinning out of control, and so it took her a second to gather her bearings. She could hear the van screeching to a stop and the distant shouts as they turned it around on the narrow street.

She pumped harder and faster, ignoring everything, including the pain from her landing, as she sprinted down one street, then another, feeling nothing but the blood singing through her, the icy wind rushing against her. She heard the earsplitting crack of a gunshot and more yelling. She cried out and ducked, but kept running just the same.

'Go, just go, don't look back.' She remembered her

track coach's words echoing in her ears. '*You lose a second every time you look back.*'

She made it to the old Laurel Springs Cemetery, her feet hitting the gravel drive now, thinking, as she dashed around tombstones and sprays of flowers, that it was somehow wrong to use a person's final resting place as a hiding spot. She slipped on the wet grass before making it to a two-story white stone mausoleum, surging through the open middle area, straight to the woods behind the cemetery. It was only when she was behind the safety of the icy trees and brush, that she allowed herself to stop, to look behind her. She crouched down, her eyes darting everywhere, her heart still slamming against her chest.

But there was nothing. No one, no sound. It was several seconds before she saw him, jogging along the gravel path, still far away, in the cemetery. He looked all around. She didn't move, didn't breathe. The van pulled along the side road and someone rolled a window down as it stopped clear in the middle of the street. The trees blocked her view of who it was, but she heard the driver say, "Let's go! Now!"

"I know she came through here! Just give me a minute. I know I can find her," he screamed.

"Get the hell in the van before someone else sees you!" the man driving the van yelled back.

Yeah, Scotlyn cheered silently. Funny how no one else seemed to be around at that late hour. No one at all.

He did, but not before turning and screaming one

more time at the empty cemetery, at the woman listening, the woman he couldn't see. "You'd better hope I never find you! Because I'll kill you. I promise, I will. I know what you look like, what you sound like! I *will* find you!"

☙☙

Scotlyn sat up, stretching her slender arms over her head. She sat for a long time, replaying the man's words, verbatim, over and over, for a long time, until they didn't seem like words anymore. She reached to her nightstand for her Albuterol inhaler and breathed deeply from it before turning her head up to the ceiling and closing her eyes, letting it do its thing. Sure, being so quiet and shy in school had made her a victim of some minor bullying, but nothing, no memory, had left quite a mark on her soul the way that man's words had. He threatened to *kill* her, no he'd *promised* to kill her.

She turned her head down and looked at her inhaler still in her hands. Despite the man's words, that haunted her like they did every morning, today felt good. Normal. Like there was nothing to fear. And maybe there wasn't. Maybe that man she'd glimpsed wouldn't make good on his word. Maybe he wouldn't find her. Maybe he wouldn't kill her if he did. Maybe he was just…gone.

Maybe.

After a while, she kicked the warm comforter away, almost reluctantly, and swung her feet onto the hardwood floor. She didn't bother making her bed and stepped over the pile of clothes in the laundry basket on her way to the bathroom, wondering if those were dirty or clean. She padded down the hall to the icy bathroom that she'd tiled in blue and white, washed her hands and face, and pulled her long, dark hair into a ponytail.

Striking, she thought to herself as she looked in the square mirror above the sink. Her eyes were dark blue with a few flecks of silver here and there. That, combined with her pale white skin and black hair had caused Raylan, her last boyfriend, to describe her as striking. She and Raylan had broken up a few weeks prior to the robbery. She'd half expected him to call her after the robbery, seeing as how it had been in the papers. But though some people had witnessed her kidnapping, no one knew her, or knew she'd escaped. She hadn't said a word about the incident, except to one person, her therapist. Thank God, she had already made the deposit that day and there had been no one in the bank she knew or who recognized her.

Scotlyn looked at herself a moment longer in the mirror, wondering if it was such a good thing to keep this to herself and Dr. Brenner. He'd commented on that a few times, but never pressured her and had always insisted that everything she told him was confidential.

Scotlyn shook her head at her reflection and let the memory of Raylan slip away as she padded through the house to her little yellow kitchen. The sun streamed in from the bay windows that overlooked her small fenced-in backyard, brightening the room even more.

One good thing, at least the robbery had given her something new to feel other than depression over yet another broken relationship. She supposed the depression was inevitable, just like fear was now, though it wasn't really that bad, she thought as she poured herself a cup of coffee. There had only been one guy in her life to leave her with a prolonged sadness she still sometimes felt, and it was a guy who'd never asked her out, never even touched her. James McIntyre. He'd moved to Laurel Springs in the middle of their junior year of high school, and like her, he was the only child of a single father. He was also quiet like her, but had an easy charm about him that allowed him to make friends easily. Maybe it was the way he could just do anything without really trying that she liked about him. He excelled at track and played soccer. He was the only person in their English class to make an A on the poem they were assigned to write. He even worked in his father's garage after school, knowing, at sixteen, just about everything his mechanic father did about cars.

Scotlyn leaned against the counter and took long, slow sips from her cup as the full memory of him returned, the memory she'd naturally run to while hiding there in the woods for hours after that white van had sped off. She remembered how she was so nervous the day they'd been paired as lab partners in Chemistry because she, of course, wasn't doing so well in the class. Any course involving numbers tripped her up. She'd get the shakes and cold sweats every time her Algebra instructor called her to the front to work a problem, especially since he'd chastised her for being unable to just "get it," and convinced her that she couldn't succeed anywhere but at a community college. But at least she knew now how untrue *that* was, even if she didn't back then. All one had to do was ask her about something intangible, something that could be interpreted, like a Georgia O'Keefe painting or a novel by one of the Bronte sisters, and she was off and running, feeling her confidence glow.

Scotlyn had initially wished she'd been paired with this handsome, dark-haired young man in one of those classes she knew inside and out, where she could actually impress him rather than fall on her face with her lack of knowledge. No, what she really liked was to watch him as he raked his hand through his dark hair or drummed his pencil against the side of his face as he listened to what the teacher was saying, much the same way she watched people at lunch. Rather than eating, she sketched them as they moved in and out of groups while she largely sat alone. People of her generation had always seemed as if they were from foreign countries, speaking languages she couldn't, and didn't care to, understand.

She knew when James moved to sit beside her that he'd find her just as stupid as she felt. But he didn't. He was good at helping her figure out the answers and actually understand the material, nodding and smiling when he could see the answers coming together in her mind. When class was over, he walked steadily beside her to English, the other class they shared, telling her his own story about growing up in Montana on his uncle's ranch, until they moved back to South Carolina, where his father had originally grown up. He asked to see her sketchpad, and admired the soft lines of her drawings. All of this—his quiet way of speaking, of listening and never interrupting as she told him about her own life—led to an almost immediate attraction and the old nervousness was replaced with a different, better one. They talked every class period, and walking together to English class became a tradition, of sorts. Then one Friday in late May, he asked if he could walk her home. She only lived about a mile from school and walked slowly with him, trying to drag it out. They chatted about their classes and classmates, and assignments, as always. He had a nervous way of laughing after saying something sometimes, the way she did. She really thought he was maybe going to ask her out for that very night. But, he never did. He just left her with that easygoing, crooked smile of his.

When he didn't come back to school after three days of being away, Scotlyn asked her Chemistry teacher about him. He informed her that James and his father had moved back to Montana that past weekend.

Scotlyn had to run to the restroom instead of going to English class, so no one would see her crying. He knew he was leaving. That was why he wanted to walk her home, why he never bothered to ask her out on a real date. He was gone, probably forever.

Scotlyn, not realizing she was half-smiling at the memory of him, took another sip of the coffee and looked at the clock on the stove—7:23. She didn't have to see Dr. Brenner until nine-thirty. She had just enough time to go for a run if she really wanted. She could feel her shoulders droop a little. A quiet morning with just her coffee and her thoughts sounded better. Or maybe she could sit at the breakfast table and paint an image of how the sun was streaming in through her bay windows. She took another sip and considered.

Dr. Brenner, at first encouraging, had lately been downright insistent that she leave the house more.

Scotlyn pulled one foot up to her back, stretching her thigh. Her legs, once so strong from all of the avid running she used to do, were now weakened to the point of frozen pain every time she dared to pound the pavement. She uncoiled her leg and looked outside. It was daylight, morning, perfectly safe. Conceding, she set her coffee on the counter and went back to her room to fish through the laundry basket. She found some yoga pants, a long-sleeved T-shirt, and a white pullover. James still lingered in her head, but she didn't mind. His memory warmed her. She still wondered if maybe she'd actually loved James, and that's why she found it so hard to let him go, even now, or maybe she felt she *could* have loved him. Whatever the case, the memory of him never really left. Even her old yearbook was creased with where she'd opened it hundreds of times to look at the only picture taken of him running track and, of course, winning the race he was running. She never told anyone, not Jane, not her father, about her feelings for James, just kept them tucked away in the back of her mind, a perfect memory she could visit when things weren't going so great. Sometimes she found herself sketching the way she saw him back then—angular cheekbones, dark hair and eyes, but then she'd feel weird and rip the drawings out of her sketchbook and throw them out, leading her to sometimes wonder if maybe he'd never left her mind because he had left her in reality. He'd left before a relationship could even begin between them. Ever since she could remember, she'd been the one to leave first, the one who could not commit, even now. She wondered if her free-spirited spitfire of a mother, a woman she'd never met, a woman who couldn't commit even to her daughter, had given that to her.

The curiosity faded as Scotlyn stuffed her backup inhaler in her pocket, found her keys and cell under a pile of unopened mail on her glass breakfast table, and checked her phone to be sure it was on and had plenty of juice since she'd forgotten to charge it the night before. If her father called her and couldn't reach her, he was likely to call the police station and hospital before showing up at her door and giving her a lecture.

Scotlyn closed and locked the door behind her just as an arctic blast rushed against her face. She shivered, zipped her pullover up to her neck, and decided just to break into a run to warm herself up faster, rather than trying to stretch. She knew she'd regret it later, but decided to deal with the consequences when they happened. She hopped down the concrete steps leading to the sidewalk and stepped into an easy, slow gait. She knew her weak lungs would slow her to a walk soon, but she'd keep up as much as she could. She turned up Church Street and passed the large First Baptist Church, with its stained glass windows and immense white pillars out front, before stopping, wondering if she should go left or right onto Main Street. Right would take her along a quiet, tree-lined route of old homes, quaint as they were when they were first built hundreds of years ago. But turning left…

Scotlyn rolled her eyes at herself. She'd turned right during her run last week. She knew she couldn't avoid turning left forever. Dr. Brenner was right. Getting through the fear would take a certain amount of head-on confrontation. The robbers were probably long gone. Really, what were the chances that, after three months, they were sitting there waiting for her to pass the bank? So, after a few seconds and a few breaths, she turned left, toward the town square. Quite a few cars were on the road despite the hour, and Scotlyn lifted her hand in greeting at each one, though she didn't know a single person who passed her. That was the way it was here. Although Scotlyn sometimes got annoyed and just wished she could focus on her run without worrying about others, most of the time she enjoyed the friendliness. It made her feel better, safer, somehow. What didn't make her feel safe, however, was what she was now approaching. She kept her head down, only looking at the large, white bank with upturned eyes and found herself picking up her pace. Her lungs went into a bit of a panic, but she concentrated on breathing, on willing them to behave.

Scotlyn sprinted across the street without looking side to side first, and wondered if she'd be able to pass that building ever again without every detail of the day coming back. She made it to the town square, with its immense, iron-gray courthouse, with about a thousand steps to the front door. Brick-faced, quaint shops surrounded the building, including a dress shop and jewelry store that had been there since before Scotlyn was born. There were also gift shops, a small one-picture theater, a sandwich shop, a Greek-Italian restaurant, a couple of law offices, and of course, her father's bookstore on the other end of the square. Scotlyn hurried past, hoping he didn't see her jogging and now wondering why she'd decided to come this route. She knew he'd ream her if he found out she was out running in the cold, with asthma. Scotlyn slowed, looking up one side of the road and down the other before crossing under the red light and turning again, picking up the pace and racing past the old Laurel Springs Cemetery with its dilapidated, yet charmingly antique wrought-iron fence as if she were running away from the scene of a crime.

She gulped down half a bottle of water when she made it back home and shed her clothes as she walked to the bathroom to run a hot shower. It soothed her muscles that were tired and sore in that nice way after a workout, causing her to stay in longer than she needed, and by the time she forced herself out, she was running late. She dried off in a hurry and flipped on the television as she rooted around, in yet another laundry basket, for some unwrinkled clothes. Her ears perked up when she heard something the newscaster was saying about some robbery that had taken place in Columbia at a precious metals warehouse. Apparently someone, or a group, had broken in at night and had stolen about half a million dollars' worth of precious metals, leaving behind no trace or hint of anything. Scotlyn set aside a long-sleeved white T-shirt and some jeans, and absentmindedly wondered if the group who did this could be the same group that robbed the bank she was in a couple of months ago. She wasn't surprised, when the newscaster closed the story with a recap on the bank robbery in Laurel Springs, and set about drying her hair. She went to grab her clothes but stopped when she passed her full-length mirror. For weeks after she escaped, she'd seen black and purple bruises covering her shoulder, hip, and leg when she passed that mirror. The stabbing, then aching, pain had kept her from sleeping on that side of her body for at least a month. She ran her hand down that shoulder and arm, past her hip. The bruises weren't there anymore, but she felt them still, and, if she looked hard enough, could still see them. Scotlyn closed her eyes and turned away. She hurriedly dressed, all the while refusing to look in that mirror again, and finished off the outfit with some low-cut black boots and a silver Celtic cross hanging from a black leather cord necklace. The necklace was one of the only things Scotlyn's mother had left behind before leaving Scotlyn and her father for good. Scotlyn didn't know if her mother had left it for her intentionally, or had just forgotten it. Scotlyn touched it now, remembering how she'd found it one summer afternoon on her dad's bureau when she was eight, saw that it had obviously been untouched in ages, and took it to him. He'd told her it was her mother's, or had been, anyway.

"I don't know why she left it," she remembered him saying as he turned it over in his hand before handing it to her with a sad smile. "But you can have it."

To this day, Scotlyn wore it almost every day.

She applied a little powder, mascara, and some lip balm and grabbed her black leather blazer as she ran out the door. Only ten minutes now to get to Dr. Brenner's and it would take at least fifteen if the traffic was good. Scotlyn was wondering how fast she could high-tail it across town without getting stopped when she threw her car into drive and raced out of her driveway, spitting gravel behind her.

She made herself slow down, though, as she got on the little four-lane road leading to Dr. Brenner's office, still running late but feeling light and happy, as if something good were about to happen. But then she passed into the outskirts of town, and the roads became narrower, the buildings sparser.

She didn't know if it was the fear that was still percolating after three months, or maybe the newscaster's report finding its way to the front of her mind again. Or maybe it was the way some spidery tree branches above suddenly cast a long shadow along the inside of her car, but something changed. She could feel her smile fall away, could hear her dad's words again, words he used so much they should've been his catchphrase. But this time, instead of dismissing them, she heeded them, over and over until they became a mantra in her mind.

'Careful. Be careful.'

Chapter 2

Tommy stared into space as he ran his fingers along the pistol on the table before him. His long, greasy brown hair hung over eyes that were fierce even when he wasn't angry, eyes that now glared with thought. Clay sat next to him, his overly muscled arms crossed over his chest. He stayed quiet, like he usually did, watching and waiting, listening and observing. Jeff, meanwhile, walked back and forth, ranting, though Tommy mostly tuned him out.

"This is our chance," Jeff went on. "We've got to get out of robbing banks. Last time was close, too close."

He kicked a chair at the opposite end of the table,

making it slide several feet before skidding and tripping. Then he kicked it again, with more force this time, until it hit the wall across the room. He breathed hard, punching his fist into his palm.

Yeah, and it's all because of you, you idiot, Tommy thought, watching him now. Jeff wasn't as large and muscled as he and Clay, but he made up for it with his ferociousness. They'd mainly brought him along to scare people, to keep them from doing something stupid.

Tommy's thoughts went back to this possible deal with Jimmy, who was sitting in the next room, awaiting their answer.

Jimmy, Tommy thought now, shaking his head. The guy was a natural-born thief. Slick, he had taken down a couple of banks with them years ago and, through some simple changes in their well-thought-out plan, had gotten them out of the bank faster and with more money. It was no wonder he'd made his way to California to work with some real-time thieves. Thievery was a small world. Word got out fast who was good, and who wasn't. Tommy and his crew weren't quite there with the good, yet. But now Jimmy was back in South Carolina, parading around like a king with all his money and making them quite the offer, one they'd be fools to refuse.

Still, Tommy thought, his mind returning to the unanswered questions. *Why now? Why us, after all these years?*

Something didn't seem right. And yet, something did, at the same time. If they started doing business with Jimmy, who knew the business inside and out and knew who he could trust, they could cut years off of waiting to work with some of the big crews, and cut loose Jeff, who was still raving incoherently.

Tommy looked at Jeff, shaking his head. Because of him, because he had been stupid enough or hung over enough to not secure his mask properly, they hadn't been able to work and hadn't had a payoff in three months. They'd had to lay low, had to put everything on hold to try and find her, to see if she'd told the police anything. Lucky for them, and for her, it looked like she hadn't talked.

Still, how could he have been so stupid? Probably *was* hung over at the time. That's what he spent most of his cut on—booze and women at the strip club, who wouldn't give him the time of day if he didn't flash hundreds like they were business cards. Tommy wouldn't care so much. He was even able to get away with giving Jeff two hundred dollars less this time, without Jeff even noticing. They'd cut him loose soon enough.

"Let's go," Tommy said, getting up from the table and replacing his gun in the holster at his back, then scratching his three-day-old beard.

"So we're going to do it, right?" Jeff asked, running up beside him like an attention-deprived puppy.

"Shut up."

Tommy could hear Jeff's breathing pick up a little and knew the little cretin was angry, but Tommy didn't care. Jeff knew better than to challenge his boss further.

They walked back into the living area and found Jimmy still sitting there in that blue chair, waiting, with one foot propped on the opposite knee. He wore a light gray suit with a white shirt underneath, but no tie—the easy California style he'd picked up living out there, Tommy supposed, and thought that *he* deserved to dress like that, to drive that black Charger that Jimmy had driven up in, to go to the best clubs, restaurants, hotels, to have probably hundreds of gorgeous women falling at his feet simply because he obviously had money. He hated living here in this crappy little house, living job to job.

"Grab us a couple of beers, Jeff," he said as he sank into a sofa opposite Jimmy, glaring right into his eyes. Jimmy kept his easy poker face, relaxed, calm. Clay remained standing.

"You want a beer?" Tommy offered.

"Take a scotch if you have it," Jimmy said.

Tommy laughed, knowing that Jimmy was showing off, in part, his new, better tastes.

"You came to the wrong place," he said. "Nothing but cheap beer here."

"I can change that," Jimmy said, brushing something away from his knee, subtly reiterating his offer.

"Why?" Tommy asked for the first time, sitting back and crossing his arms over his chest, again glaring at his former friend. He thought "former," though they were never that close and had never actually had a falling out. Jimmy had just moved on to bigger and better things, and that was just enough to make Tommy hate him for the past several years.

"Thought you might benefit from doing a few less-conspicuous, higher-paying jobs," Jimmy said, then called to Jeff in the kitchen: "I will take one of those beers."

"Why you doin' this for us?" Tommy asked, nodding once in Jimmy's direction.

Jimmy took a swig from his beer before setting it on the coffee table and leaning forward. "Happened to be back in town. My father's starting up his business here again. I'm helping him out a little, you know—part of my cover."

"Hmm," Tommy said, waiting for Jimmy to go on.

"Call it payback," Jimmy said. "You guys were pretty good to me when I was getting started."

Tommy raised his eyebrows and took a sip of his own beer. That was true enough, though he spotted flattery when he heard it. Didn't mean it didn't work, though.

"What's the mark?" Tommy asked. "And the cut?"

"The mark is in North Carolina," Jimmy said. "I'll get the details to you later."

"How much later?" Clay asked, his voice as burly as his stature.

Damn it, Tommy thought, cursing Clay. *Don't let him know how desperate we are*. If Jimmy knew how far behind they were on bills and payments, he'd have the upper hand even more so than he did now.

Jimmy turned to him, holding his stare for a second, before saying, "Soon."

"The cut," Jeff repeated. "He asked you the cut."

"Twenty percent," Jimmy said, pointing at Tommy, and then "Eighty," as he pointed at his own chest.

"Hmm," Tommy thought out loud. He held up the amber bottle, studied it as the sunlight streaming in from the window shone through it. "The value?"

"Two million and change, minus ten percent of that to my fence."

"Twenty percent of…1.8 then?" Tommy asked, still looking at the bottle, hoping his excitement didn't show. Jeff did that just fine.

"Hell, yeah," Jeff said, jumping up and punching at the air.

Tommy looked at Jeff. He sat his ass back down.

"Three hundred sixty thousand, just like that," Jimmy said, sitting back in his chair, still relaxed. He negotiated numbers like that all the time.

"Make it thirty percent. And we have a deal right now."

Jimmy laughed, still keeping eye contact. Tommy didn't bat an eye and didn't laugh.

"No way can I do that," Jimmy said and Tommy

wanted to rip his head off. "I can maybe push it to twenty-two."

"Twenty-five," Tommy countered.

Jimmy was quiet, but not hesitating. "Twenty-three. Final offer. It's that or nothing."

Tommy tried to calculate that in his mind. Twenty-three percent was well over four hundred thousand, he figured. His cut alone would be two hundred thousand. And he could sure use that money. It'd sure be a good start at a better life.

"Fine," he said, and he and Jimmy reached forward at the same time to shake hands.

Jimmy stood up and put on sunglasses.

"Good seeing you again Clay," he said. Clay said nothing, only watched him. "Jeff," Jimmy said in closing.

Jeff's beady eyes flashed and Jimmy smiled as he began making his way to the front door.

"Now all I've got to do is kill her and we're home free," Jeff said and Tommy closed his eyes as Jimmy stopped and, almost as an afterthought, turned around.

They waited.

Jimmy never took hostages or victims. He'd even tweaked their robbery plans years ago to avoid that on every job. The guy just had a soft heart, couldn't pull the trigger, even at his own enemy.

"Her?" he asked, looking pointedly at Tommy. "What's he talking about?"

Tommy sighed, brought his hands together in front

of him, and rubbed them together a few times. He thought about lying to Jimmy, but then again, the truth might convince him to help them out more. So, he told Jimmy everything. Jimmy just stared at him with the sunglasses still over his eyes.

When Tommy finished the story, Jimmy looked up at the cracked ceiling. "Cut to three months later," he said, as if retelling himself the story. "You've found her."

"Clay?" Tommy said to his right hand man.

Clay said nothing, only retrieved his phone from his pocket. He pressed a few buttons before rising and handing it to Jimmy.

"Clay took those just this morning," Tommy said as Jimmy looked at the pictures in silence. "Seems she's gotten brave enough to jog along the very path of the bank. Then she led him all the way back to her little house."

Jimmy handed Clay the phone and then looked at Tommy. "What's your plan?"

"What are you, deaf?" Jeff screeched. "I told you, I'm going to kill her!"

Tommy held up a hand in Jeff's general direction. It was obvious from Jimmy's still-stony expression that he didn't like Jeff, or what he was saying. A part of Tommy was paranoid enough to do away with this girl, but he would be damned if he let Jeff ruin this chance at better work and a better life because he couldn't keep his stupid mouth shut.

But before he could react, Jimmy responded with, "I see," and scratched the side of his face. Then he put his hands in his pockets and looked at Jeff, sunglasses still over his eyes.

Tommy felt like he was standing on the edge of a cliff. No matter what direction he took, it would be the wrong one.

But then Jimmy surprised him. "Perhaps there's another way of dealing with her."

Tommy felt his face break into the smallest of half smiles. Ah, a bargaining chip. Jimmy never could stand to see a victim hurt. With this in mind, he said, "I think Jeff's pretty clear on this. She's been too scared to talk until now. But she *will* break—eventually. She has to die."

Tommy wouldn't let that happen, of course. If possible, he also liked to keep the body count down, and after three months, she probably wasn't going to talk, but Jimmy didn't have to know that, now did he?

"I recognize her," Jimmy said. "I knew her when I lived here for a few months in high school. She had quite the crush on me back then."

Tommy's mouth formed into a full smile. Well, well, well, what were the odds? "And?" he asked.

"And, maybe I could use that, probe her a little, play her a while until she trusts me. You know how women are when they fall in love."

"Get her to *confide* in you, is that it?" Tommy asked.

"See if she really remembers anything, saw anything. There's no reason she has to die—"

Tommy half laughed. Jeff's eyes were raging now that they were inching his prey right out from under him. Tommy thought for a moment, knowing Jimmy could pull this off. Jimmy was practically a human lie detector, knew just who he could trust and who he couldn't in the world of criminals. Another reason Tommy had to be careful around him.

"It'll cost you," Tommy said, finally.

Jimmy waited.

"That little robbery at the metals factory outside of Columbia—I assume that was you?"

Jimmy just smiled, slowly this time.

"Fifty percent of your takings from that."

Jimmy laughed to himself and shook his head. Tommy pressed his finger in the wound.

"Jeff," he said. "You want to enlighten Jimmy on the tactics you use to kill people?"

Jimmy held up his hand, stopping Jeff. "Fine. But I don't give you the mark on this new job until I ensure she knows nothing and that she's safe."

"Fine," Tommy said.

"And you don't interfere," Jimmy said. The smile was long gone.

"Long as you keep us updated."

Jimmy paused but said, "Fair enough."

He turned, but Tommy stopped him with one final

question, just for fun. "How do you know we aren't going to kill her when you skip back to California?"

"I have ways," Jimmy said. "I'll be around a while. And I'll be watching." He turned to Jeff. "So will my contacts. Anything happens to her…"

He let the last thought hang in the air.

Tommy grinned then, knowing that Jimmy had a thing for this girl, knowing they could use her any way they wanted and Jimmy would bend.

Yup, Tommy thought. *There's our collateral. You're a smart man, Jimmy, but you're a real idiot sometimes, too.*

Jeff, oblivious to what Tommy was thinking, clenched his jaw. He was an attack dog on a chain, just waiting to unleash his rage, though his master wouldn't let him.

Tommy almost gave him the go ahead to try something with Jimmy, knowing that, even though Jimmy had a soft spot for female victims, he could snap Jeff's arm and then his neck before Jeff would even know what had happened. *It would've been a nice show*, Tommy thought to himself as he watched Jimmy half wave and then turn to walk out the front door.

Chapter 3

"You're late," Scotlyn's father said as she pushed open the heavy glass door to the bookshop, the little bell jingling as it always did when someone entered. She could smell some foreign coffee he'd brewed for the customers. A classical song was playing over the speakers, the volume turned low.

"Sorry," she said. "Had Dr. Brenner's this morning." She passed the shelf displaying different newspapers and magazines and the center table, her boots making echoing sounds on the hardwood floor. He was sitting behind the long oak counter upon which sat the register at one end, and at the other, a large coffee maker flanked by small

Styrofoam cups and a glass bowl filled with little cream and sugar packets.

She was supposed to charge twenty-five cents each time someone got a cup of coffee, as the little homemade sign beside the pot indicated, but every time someone offered her the money, she couldn't help but wave it away. She knew her father would kill her if he knew she'd been doing that.

"Oh, right," he said. "Wednesday. How'd it go?"

"Good," she said, and she was right.

Though Dr. Brenner never smiled, he also never hurried and had a calm, easygoing nature that put her at ease. She left his office feeling the way she always did, better and calmer, like she now knew what she needed in order to make it through the day.

She stopped at one of the display tables to straighten a book that had been turned askew. "What kind of coffee is that?"

"Kenyan," he said. "Bold roast."

"Thought it was different," she said, and then turned down one of the aisles on her way to the back office. "Be right back."

"Bring that shipment up when you come," he said. "I forgot to this morning."

Scotlyn just said "okay," but she knew he hadn't forgotten. He probably couldn't lift it. Though her dad wasn't even into his fifties—he and her mother were barely out of high school when Scotlyn was born—he was already having awful back pain. He refused to see a doctor about it and refused to admit it was even happening, even hiding the pain pills she knew he took several times a day. She knew it was the part in him that hated getting older that was refusing to let him admit to this, but she really wished he'd get it checked out.

Scotlyn walked down the three steps to the tiny office, dropped her purse on the desk that took up most of the space in it, and hung her jacket on the chair. She picked up the box that was still on the floor, seeing why her father couldn't lift them. They must've been hardbacks. She heaved the books up to the front, noticing that, despite the pain he was obviously in, her father was still in remarkable shape. He was tall, with the same deep blue eyes as Scotlyn, and a few lines around them and his mouth, and salt and pepper hair, making him look regal and distinguished.

"Thanks, sweetie," he said, opening the box and beginning to scan the books.

"No problem," she said. "I'll set them up in the window display this afternoon."

"Replace the cookbooks with these," he said. "Not the new fiction order. Those are still moving pretty good."

"Sure," she said.

They always kept a small display in the front window of their newest arrivals, and he always left it to Scotlyn to set it up.

He didn't say anything more, and she could see that something was coming.

Oh no, she thought, taking note of the uneasiness now beginning to settle around them.

"Did I see you out running this morning?" he asked, still scanning the books but turning his eyes up to look at her.

Scotlyn froze for a moment, wondering if she should just lie about it. It would be easier. She wouldn't have to try to deal with his looks and tone of voice that was sure to follow and last the rest of the day. But she knew she couldn't. She'd lied to her father maybe three times in her twenty-nine years and he'd always found out the truth. She hated the feeling she got when she did, anyway, and decided it wasn't worth it. She just half smiled, sheepishly, and felt her face go hot.

Her father sighed, shaking his head as he finished scanning the books. "You know what the doctor said about your asthma," he said.

"Yeah, he said it was fine as long as I took it easy and had my backup inhaler, which I did," Scotlyn said, a bit too cheerfully, to keep the peace.

"Hmm," he said, his voice not matching her cheerfulness. "I really wish you'd just walk instead of run. You do a lot more damage to your body than just your respiratory system when you run."

Scotlyn shrugged, willing the conversation to hurry to its ending.

"But," he conceded, finishing up scanning the last book. "It's your life." He put the books on the shelf behind the counter, not looking at Scotlyn. Suddenly, he stretched. "Looks like it's going to be a slow day."

Scotlyn, still dwelling on their last conversation, needed just a moment before responding. "Oh," she said. "Yeah, I guess."

"Think I'll go sit in that comfortable chair in the office," he said. "Work on the books. You mind starting in on the inventory for the art and science sections? I did the fiction already this morning."

"No, I'll go ahead and start on that," she said, and he handed her the lists with the science and art books on them.

"Thanks," he said. "Not really feeling up to par today."

"You should see a doctor," she said, looking at the list, turning the previous argument around on him. If he wanted to play this game, he had to be all in.

"Ah, I'm fine," he said, waving his hand at her.

He hadn't seen a doctor in probably twenty years, even when he had a horrible flu several years ago that had kept him in bed for over a week.

"Famous last words," she called after him, and he shook his finger at her without turning around.

Scotlyn sighed, half smiling, and took the list to the art section to get to work. The worse her father felt, the more work she did around here, though she didn't mind it. She liked the atmosphere that he'd set up in the store, liked the fact that it wasn't just a job, but her father's legacy that she was helping to preserve. Five years ago, when she was living in Arizona, she got a call from him. She'd been at the Grand Canyon, sketching it from all possible angles, though each one looked the same in her pictures. He'd asked, but not begged her to come back for a while to help him run his store.

"Eleven hours a day, six days a week is just starting to be a bit much," he'd said.

He didn't sound good when he spoke and that's what ultimately convinced Scotlyn to come back as soon as she quit her job, packed up as much of her stuff as she could, and sold off the rest. She drove for almost two days straight, plowing through the places she'd stopped to stay in on her travels, simply because they'd seemed like nice places. When she arrived in the town she couldn't get away from fast enough two years earlier, she knew she'd be staying a while, probably forever. She'd had her fun traveling from place to place, had even sold a couple of drawings to some small galleries along the way, but now her father needed her.

The bell sounded just then and Scotlyn turned just in time to see her best friend's blonde head duck to the right and make a beeline for the fiction and literature shelves. Scotlyn raised an eyebrow, wondering what was up, and shelved the clipboard to mark her place. She walked over to the literature section and peered at Jane, her hand still resting on one of the shelves. Jane was searching intently in the F section, unaware of Scotlyn standing not five feet away.

"Can I help you?" Scotlyn asked, half grinning.

Jane glanced up with an exhausted and panicked look on her face. "You don't sell *Cliff's Notes*, by chance, do you?"

Scotlyn shook her head, still half-smiling. Jane rolled her eyes and placed her hands on her hips. "We're reading *The Great Gatsby* in my American Lit class and I can't get it. I need help. You don't by chance remember it from college, do you?"

While Scotlyn had gone to Methodist College two towns away, Jane had gotten married straight out of high school to Albert, a man thirty-seven years old to her eighteen. Scotlyn had gone to the wedding, though, despite their being lifelong friends, she hadn't been a bridesmaid. That honor had been granted to Albert's three sisters, the first of many controlling acts he'd held over Jane. They'd gone on to live in a doublewide trailer on his parents' property, not the cute two-bedroom home in town that Jane had had her eye on. She spent her days cleaning, cooking, doing laundry, and tending to the kids when they came along, instead of going to college. She'd seemed happy enough at the wedding, smiling and calling the balding and pudgy Albert "honey," but Scotlyn couldn't help but see just a tiny trace in Jane's smile that said, "What have I done?"

What *had* she done, exactly? Scotlyn wanted to ask her that very question, but she already knew the answer. Jane had grown up in a small home, the middle child, stuck between a perfect princess and an even more perfect prince. Jane was the one who never did anything right, despite her sweet nature and near-perfect grades. Albert was the first man to show her the affection she desperately craved, probably because he was closing in on forty and wanted a young wife to make him feel younger and give him children, and Jane had done so. Exactly ten months after the wedding, she'd had her first child, a hell-raising boy named Albert Jr., and then a girl, Ellen, eighteen months after that.

It was only a year earlier that Jane had filed for divorce. Albert had barely put up a fight, was probably too drunk to notice. Scotlyn was really surprised it hadn't happened earlier than that, but Jane tended to stick things out, to work at something and try to make it fit until it broke, or until she did, whichever came first. Scotlyn was relieved for Jane when she ended the marriage. Scotlyn talked her father into renting his father's old millhouse to Jane for a much lower rate than he usually charged his tenants. Now, Jane was going to Methodist on a full scholarship but seemed to be intent on losing it by trying to read the *Cliff's Notes* version of a book she'd been assigned.

"Why don't you ask your professor for help?" Scotlyn said. "Or better yet—" She grabbed a copy of the novel off the shelf and held it up to Jane. "Just read the book. It isn't that long and it's not hard. In fact, it's pretty good."

Jane waved the book away. "Hey, not everyone's an English major like you, honey. Besides, I've already got a copy."

"English minor," Scotlyn corrected and re-shelved the book. They started walking toward the front of the store.

"Whatever," Jane said, then, "I don't know. The language in the book is so hard to get through."

"It's a love story," Scotlyn said, appealing to Jane's romantic nature.

Jane was a sucker for love stories. She could always devour about three romance novels a week in school. Scotlyn even remembered when they'd seen *Titanic* together. Immediately after it was over, Jane declared she was naming her firstborn son Jack Dawson.

Jane's eyes partially lit up as they had a seat in the deep armchairs near the front display. "Doesn't seem that way," she said. "So far it's just about this guy visiting his rich cousin. When does the good part happen?"

Scotlyn laughed. "Soon."

"I don't know," Jane said. "Maybe I'll just go to the library and look up a summary online. They made a movie, too, didn't they?"

"Yeah, a few. When did you get so lazy?" Scotlyn teased, remembering Jane's relentless studying in school.

Jane didn't laugh like she used to all the time and drummed the calluses on her hands, courtesy of the years she'd spent cleaning the doublewide. "Albert zapped all my energy."

Scotlyn felt her smile drop away.

"You ever hear anything from his lawyer?" she asked, treading carefully.

Jane shrugged. "He didn't contest the divorce. Looks like I'll get child support, too, along with the monthly payments."

"That's good news," Scotlyn said.

"Yeah."

"It'll help out with the kids."

"Yup."

Scotlyn looked down, wanting to say more but not knowing what to say to this girl before her who'd taken the time to befriend and understand her when no one else had.

She sat back in the chair and crossed her legs. "Need me to watch the kids or anything tonight so you can do some homework?" she asked, feeling the need to offer something, some kind of help, but inwardly cringing at the memory of the last time she babysat Albert, Jr. It had taken her days to scrub off the crayon marks he'd left all over her living room walls and he'd ripped three of her drawings to shreds before demanding, then screaming for, chocolate cake for dinner.

"No, they're with Albert's mom this week."

Scotlyn tried not to look relieved. "Want to hang out?"

Jane shook her head. "I'll be reading that book well into the wee hours of the morning as it is."

"I could stop at Redford's and get you a hotdog," she offered, naming the fast food joint local only to Laurel Springs.

Jane finally laughed. "All right, a girl's got to eat. But I'll meet you there around seven. If you come over, I'll be too tempted to chitchat and I'll end up wasting a bunch of time."

"Deal," Scotlyn said.

"Okay," Jane said, getting up and sighing, rubbing her palms on her jeans. "*Gatsby* awaits. I'll see you tonight."

"The American Dream," Scotlyn said just before Jane reached the door.

Jane turned around. "What?"

"The American Dream," Scotlyn repeated. "That's one of the big themes in the book, as is hopeless romantics."

"Hopeless romantics," Jane said, as if she'd never before heard the words. She raised her eyebrows once before waving to Scotlyn and leaving the store.

It wasn't until around three that afternoon that she had her next customer of the day. She was on her hands and knees, adjusting the new display up front when the bell rang. She said "Hi" without looking up from her work, and a voice—quiet and masculine—returned the greeting, followed by footsteps falling slowly to the back of the store. It wasn't until Scotlyn looked up that she felt a hot, stinging in her cheeks that seemed to run through her shoulders and into her chest.

Oh my word, she thought. She didn't know how she knew it was him, but she did. She could only see him from the back, could only see dark jeans and an untucked black and red plaid button-up shirt and disheveled dark hair that was long, almost to his shoulders. He turned slightly, reaching out, taking a book from the shelf, and flipping through it before replacing it and reaching for another, looking for something in particular, obviously. He replaced that one and moved toward another shelf slowly and easily.

James, Scotlyn thought, her heart starting to gallop in her chest. Was it him? How could it be? What was he doing back here?

The man squatted, reaching for another book. Scotlyn seemed to freeze in place as she studied him, the way he moved lithely yet with purpose, like an athlete. Like James.

She suddenly realized that he would probably feel her watching him in just a second, so she moved quickly to the counter. She paced back and forth in the same spot a couple of times. It wouldn't be too obvious if she went over and asked if he needed help, would it? That would be the right thing to do, wouldn't it? As an employee, she'd only be helping a customer? She took a breath, pushed her hair behind her ears, and made a move to where he was. She had to know if it was him, though she had no idea what she'd do when she found out.

Just an employee helping a customer, she reminded herself over and over as she walked on shaky legs to the row he was still on. She suddenly grabbed a book from a previous shelf to look casual, to complete the ruse.

He'd resumed standing and was looking at another book this time, though she couldn't tell what it was.

"Uh," she said, her voice shaky, her tone barely audible. *Speak up, damn it!* "Do you need any help?"

He looked up, though not at her at first. He turned slowly, giving her full access to his angular cheekbones and green eyes that were kind yet pensive at the same time, eyes that looked straight into her. He looked at her for a moment without saying anything, like he knew her, too, but couldn't quite place her. He smiled, crookedly, then, and said, "Hey, Scotlyn."

Oh, my word, he's good-looking.

Scotlyn could feel her face break into a smile, too, though she still felt awkward and nervous. If he was, he didn't show it. He just replaced the book, came over to where she was, and pulled her into a hug. Scotlyn's breath caught as she felt the warmth of his chest against hers, but she soon relaxed and returned the hug, realizing he'd never hugged her, never so much as touched her before. He'd just been a boy she'd had a few interesting conversations with, a boy who ended up walking her home one day after school. Yet, here they were, almost fifteen years later, hugging one another as if they were the oldest of friends.

"You look really good," he said, releasing her.

"Oh, thanks. You do too," she said, feeling her face blush, not wanting him to think that was a come-on of some kind.

He didn't seem to notice, or mind, if he did think that because all he said was, "Thanks. This your store?"

"Yes. Well, sort of," she said. "My dad owns it, is grooming me to take over one day…" She rolled her eyes and trailed off.

"What've you been up to since school?" she asked.

He shrugged, as if that were all the answer she needed. "Worked on my uncle's ranch for a while, traveled some…"

He was leaving out large bits, obviously, but Scotlyn didn't ask him about that. They were strangers again, and though their hug had done away with most of the nervousness, some of it had returned now that they were standing apart again.

"You been working here since finishing up school?" he asked, taking the book off the shelf again, though still looking at her.

"No," Scotlyn said, shaking her head. "I actually traveled a bit, too, but Dad needed me to come back a few years ago. He's not doing so good. His back."

Why was she telling him all of this? She shrugged.

"I'm sorry," James said, though he'd never once met her father.

Scotlyn smiled in gratitude. "So what brings you all the way back here?"

"Actually, *my* dad," he said.

Scotlyn raised her eyebrows.

"Yeah, he's starting up his garage here again and called, asking if I'd like to help get things started, at least until he has the means to hire a few people."

"Oh," Scotlyn said, trying not to smile too giddily at the thought that he might be in town for a while.

"That's why I'm here," he said, holding up a book on car engines. "I'm a bit rusty. Haven't worked on anything in years."

"Oh," Scotlyn said again. "Well, I'm sure you'll pick it up again pretty easily. You were so good at everything you did..."

She blushed as she trailed off once again. She always seemed to say things that went a little too far in awkward moments. He didn't seem to notice, though, or didn't acknowledge it if he did, and Scotlyn suddenly remembered that was one of the things she liked best about this guy before her.

He made a move to walk to the front of the store, though not in a hurry, and she followed suit.

"So, you go to college after high school?" he asked.

"I did," Scotlyn said. "Methodist. Majored in

Business and Art, minored in English. Dad couldn't have been happier because he thought that made the perfect combination for me to start running this place when I graduated. But..."

He was still looking at her as they made it to the front of the store and she went around the counter while he stayed on the other end.

"You wanted to travel," he finished for her.

She nodded, remembering telling him that moments before.

"You get to see the Grand Canyon?"

She grimaced at him. How did he know—

"I remember you saying in high school how much you always wanted to see it," he said, as if reading her thoughts.

Scotlyn could feel her eyes widen slightly.

"Wow," she said. "I'm surprised you remember that. It was ages ago."

James half-smiled. "I remember a lot."

"Well, yeah, I did see the Grand Canyon, though I didn't go there first. I stopped a few places along the way—New Orleans, San Antonio, Las Vegas."

"Got to see a bit of the country, then."

"Yeah," she said. "I even sold a couple of drawings."

"Nice," he said. "Yeah, I remember you always drawing something in your notebooks."

His eyes moved to the wall behind her, scanning it until he saw a drawing she'd done of some horses grazing in a pasture. She remembered the day she saw those horses, just minding their own business, their heads gracefully reaching to the ground as they made a feast on grass. There was something beautiful in the lines of their muscles, the fall of their manes, the way their tails swished elegantly from one side to the other. Scotlyn had just pulled her car over to the side of the road and immediately gone to work drawing them.

"You do that one?" he asked.

She nodded.

"I like that," he said. "Maybe I'll buy one from you, too."

She laughed, thinking it a joke, but he winked at her as he set his book on the counter, a gesture that almost froze her where she was. She swallowed as she took the book and scanned it.

"It's nine-thirty-three," she said, looking at the screen displaying the price.

James pulled a wad of bills from his pocket and began thumbing through them.

Whoa, she thought, trying not to stare. *Who carries that much cash?*

What did he do that he earned enough just to carry that much around?

"So, did you end up going to college?" she fished, looking for the answer to her questions.

He shrugged, still looking down. "No, like I said I worked on my uncle's ranch. Did some construction work. I actually may have been near New Orleans when you were there."

She smiled, but didn't ask when he was there because she liked the idea that they could have been so close, but didn't know it.

He finally found a ten and handed it to her between two fingers. She couldn't help noticing his hands as she took the money from him. They still had that nice, oblique bone structure, but were a bit roughened now, like he'd been working a long time. She focused on giving him his change, her hand brushing his as she did so. Bagging his book, she slid it across the counter to him. She was starting to get a little panicked and sad that he was leaving and she didn't know when she'd see him again.

She began thinking about an excuse to bring her car in to his father's garage when he said, "Hey, what are you doing tonight? Do you have plans?"

She could feel her heart start to flutter again and had to remind herself to take a breath. She smiled and was about to tell him no, she didn't have plans, when Jane all of a sudden came to mind. *Damn it.*

"Oh," she said, shutting her eyes. "I, uh—" *He's going to think I don't want to go. Think!* "I—I do tonight," she said, but hurried on with, "But I don't tomorrow."

Please, please, please, she thought.

"Well, it's just that I just got back into town," he

said. "Haven't seen many people again yet, and wouldn't mind just catching up—"

"Oh," she said, nodding, fully aware that he hadn't officially asked her. She surely wasn't going to ask him. She'd made that mistake once with a guy from Methodist. They'd met at the library one day.

He'd called her up one Thursday evening and had started the conversation by asking what she was doing that weekend.

When she'd eagerly said she had no plans and could go out, he'd replied with, "I'm going to the *beach*! I've never been there before! Isn't that cool?"

Scotlyn hadn't been able to respond and had avoided the library for two weeks after that.

"Would you mind if I stopped by when you got off?" James now asked, bringing her back to him. "Or, we could meet somewhere."

"No, that's fine," she said, trying to force the grin on her face to a small smile. "I close up at six and it'll take me just a little while to finish things up, so if you want to get here about six-thirty."

He nodded once, smiling, and started to back away. "I'll be here." He turned around and put some sunglasses on, but before pushing the door open with his back, he said, "I'm glad I ran into you."

"Me too," she said. She waited until she saw him walk down the street before screaming, giggling, and bouncing up and down a couple of times.

Her father came running from the back. "What the devil?" he asked.

"Oh, sorry," she said, jumping again, still giggling a little. "I just—uh—"

Her father stood before her, waiting.

"I ran into someone from high school just now."

"Oh, lord," he said. "Must've been a boy."

"Well, he's a man, now," she said, taking a cloth and wiping down the counter, subconsciously swaying her hips and shoulders a little as she did. "James McIntyre."

"McIntyre," her father repeated. "That's not Sam McIntyre's boy, is it?"

Scotlyn looked up, thinking. "I don't know," she admitted. "He's a mechanic, has a garage."

She hoped that her father didn't hate James's father for anything. It would ruin her time with James, if only just a little, if he did. Her father didn't give her a clue at first, just stared into space, thinking.

"Oh, yeah," he said finally. "Quiet guy, but damn good with cars, even when we were kids. He could take the engine, out of anything, apart and put it right back together again. He's back in town?"

"Yeah," she said, smiling again, now with relief.

"Good," he said, turning back toward the office. "We could use a good mechanic around here."

Scotlyn smiled, folding and replacing the cloth in a random drawer.

"Wait a minute," he said, rounding the corner again.

"This James kid, I never met him. You went to school with him?"

"Yeah, he and his dad came to live here for a few months during my junior year and then they went back to Montana."

"Montana?" he asked, as if she'd mentioned some place in a sci-fi show.

She nodded.

"Huh," he said. "You like him?"

Scotlyn shrugged, though she could feel herself blushing again.

"Maybe I'll run by Sam's garage, see if I can get a look at him."

"Dad," Scotlyn pleaded and warned at the same time. "You're going to make me have an attack right here in the store."

He surprised her by laughing. "Just kidding, hon. But if you do start up with dating him, I'd like to meet him."

"Okay," Scotlyn promised, but didn't mention going out with James the following evening. Her father had specifically said "dating" and neither she nor James had called their outing a date. She rubbed the back of her neck, looked down at the counter, and felt happier than she had in a long time.

∽ح∾

As soon as James rounded the corner, he pulled out

his cellular and dialed the number he now knew by heart. When Tommy answered, all James said was, "I've made contact."

"Already?" Tommy said approvingly. "Good. Move pretty fast, don't you?"

James didn't answer, just closed the phone and replaced it in his pocket.

"Jerk," he muttered under his breath as he came back into the street and made his way to his car.

Chapter 4

Scotlyn didn't see any point in going home before meeting Jane, so she stayed at the store until she had to leave. She was still a little uncomfortable driving around or being out alone at night, so she ensured that the lamp on the front counter and the street light were on before leaving.

Redford's wasn't very far, only a couple of streets over, but Jane was already there, parked under the giant neon man holding a tray with a burger on it, leaning against her little blue Escort. She waved when she saw Scotlyn.

Scotlyn grinned back and nodded once, still a little

overly happy, which was starting to annoy even her.

"Wow, you look great," Jane said when Scotlyn got out of the car.

"You just saw me a few hours ago," Scotlyn said, double-checking her car door to be sure it was locked.

"Yeah, but something's different," Jane said as they fell into pace beside one another, walking across the parking lot, brightly lit from the florescent lights shining through the windows that encircled the restaurant.

Jane continued with, "You have this…I don't know…starry look to you. Did you meet a guy?"

Leave it to Jane to think it's romance-related, Scotlyn thought, though her friend just happened to be right.

Scotlyn opened the door, letting Jane walk ahead of her. Jane continued to give her little a Cheshire Cat grin as they walked toward the front of the restaurant, ordered two hotdog plates, filled their cups at the soda fountain, and had a seat in one of the red plastic booths.

"So, are you going to tell me or am I going to just have to stare at you all night?" Jane finally asked.

"Okay," Scotlyn said, admittedly eager to tell her best friend the news. "Do you remember James McIntyre?"

Jane thought for a minute then said out loud, "Tall guy, dark hair, played soccer and ran track? Was only here a few months?"

Scotlyn nodded.

"Yeah, I remember you had quite a thing for him," Jane said, raising her eyebrow suggestively.

Scotlyn rolled her eyes, suddenly annoyed.

"*What*?" Jane asked, her tone still playful but with a defensive edge now. "You used to talk about him all the time. It was a little obvious."

Scotlyn paused, her hotdog midway to her mouth. "Oh, no. You think he knew? How many other people knew?"

It was Jane's turn to roll her eyes. "You know how high school kids are. Two people of the opposite sex spend any amount of time together and immediately everyone asks if they're 'going together.'"

Scotlyn half-nodded. A few people, some of whom she'd never even met, had asked her that very thing about her and James. But she'd always told them the truth, no.

"You *were* kind of lit up after English class that whole year, kind of like you are now, but I never heard anyone say, 'Scotlyn has the hots for James,' or anything. You just seemed really happy. Of course, I knew all along because I know *you*."

"Of course," Scotlyn said, remembering how Jane had probed her, generally at first, then specifically about James. Scotlyn had never said a thing, though, even to her most trusted friend.

For some reason, she hadn't wanted to let slip that secret, even to Jane. It was like an old picture or a letter she kept tucked away in a drawer, one that was only for her, and revealing it to someone else would ruin something about it. Or she'd find out that James just wasn't interested and she'd rather live with the hope that he might be than the reality that he wasn't.

"So, I guess he's the reason you're so lit up again?"

Scotlyn laughed a little and dipped a fry into some ketchup. "Yeah, I guess he is. He came by the bookstore today."

"*Really*?" Jane asked, perking up like Scotlyn had mentioned a celebrity. "You're sure it was him?"

"Positive," Scotlyn answered.

"He still as hot as he was in high school?"

Scotlyn really laughed then. "Even hotter, probably."

When Scotlyn didn't elaborate, Jane hit the table with both hands. "So come on, tell me!"

Scotlyn told Jane about how they'd talked for a while, how he was back in town to help his dad, and how he'd asked her out. She could feel her cheeks burning a little as she told her friend that last part.

"Well, you should go. You should *definitely* go."

"*Definitely*?" Scotlyn repeated.

"Yes!" Jane said. "This could so be a sign—"

Scotlyn rolled her eyes. Jane and her "signs."

"Hey, say what you will, but when Albert proposed, you remember how we just tried to go off and elope and we couldn't find a notary public to save our lives?"

"Yeah, so? You ended up having a nice wedding at First Baptist."

"Whatever. That was a sign that we never should've gotten married! And maybe James reappearing all of a sudden…" Jane trailed off and stared dreamily into space as she put the story together in her mind. "Maybe he's your one true love and it just wasn't meant to be in high school. You just needed time to grow and mature and find yourself, like…like Daisy and Benjamin did in *The Curious Case of Benjamin Button*, but you're ultimately meant to be together—"

"Okay," Scotlyn said, waving her hands, pleading with her friend to stop. "I'm already way too excited about this and you saying all of this is just going to make it worse. He's probably going to leave town again, soon. We might not see each other again after this one night. He didn't even call it a date."

Jane sat back, pretending to pout, but then lit up again. "Maybe *that's* your destiny, to just have one small, but meaningful moment together every few years, like—"

"Oh, stop it," Scotlyn said, reaching for her Coke and taking a sip.

Jane shrugged. "Okay. But you *are* nuts about this guy and the possibility that he may be about you, too, should be explored."

She pointed a fry at Scotlyn as she spoke, while Scotlyn just shook her head, trying to dismiss the thought and make her friend be quiet, which she did.

"You know," Scotlyn said. "F. Scott Fitzgerald wrote the story of *The Curious Case of Benjamin Button*."

Jane dropped her face a little and stared at Scotlyn. "*What*?"

Scotlyn just laughed, knowing that would put an end to the conversation. Still, curiosity got the better of her later that evening and when she got home, she couldn't help taking out her laptop and looking James up on Facebook, but he wasn't there. Nothing even came up when she did a Google search of his name. Feeling a tad like a stalker, she put the computer away and dressed for bed early. She didn't get much sleep, but at least it wasn't because of nightmares, she thought as she sat on the deck before dawn the next morning with a blanket wrapped around her and a cup of coffee at her side, sketching the way the moon still hovered in the light blue of the morning sky.

She obsessed over what to wear, wanting to look casual but not underdressed, pretty but not overdone. She finally decided on a fitted blue sweater that brought out her eyes and was cut just low enough to show off the prominence of her slender neck and collarbone. She took the time to blow dry and straighten her hair, though she rarely washed it two days in a row, and packed up her makeup so she could reapply before he got there.

She didn't get nervous until that evening, though, close to six. Her dad hadn't even come in today, had called to tell her some things that needed to be done and said he was going fishing, but she knew better. He probably just didn't feel up to coming in. Her thoughts were confirmed when she took him some soup and a grilled cheese sandwich and found him sitting on the sofa, watching a basketball game.

"Thought you were going fishing," she said as she closed the front door behind her.

"Hey, who's watching the store?" he said, turning slightly from his perch in front of the television.

Scotlyn stepped over a pile of newspapers, observing how she'd inherited her father's cleaning habits, or lack thereof, and sat by him, just barely dodging a coffee stain that had been there for years. She held up the bag of food. "It'll be all right for an hour," she said. "This is the slowest part of the day, you know that. Anyway, I thought you might be hungry."

"Thanks," he said, taking the bag of food.

"When was the last time Mrs. Simmons came by to clean?" she asked, surveying the shoes on the carpeted floor that hadn't been vacuumed in ages, the dust on the oak coffee table and bookshelves, and the dirty dishes across the way in the kitchen sink.

"Thursday," he answered.

She waited.

"October thirteenth."

"Dad," Scotlyn said. No wonder he'd wanted to come to her house for Thanksgiving, Christmas, and New Year's Day.

"She's been sick," he went on. "Couldn't come by for a while and I don't feel right asking her."

"Well, you should've called me, or Merry Maids."

"No." He shook his head, taking a bite of the sandwich. "Ain't gonna have a stranger messin' around my house."

Scotlyn sighed, removing her coat and shaking her head. She got up and headed for the kitchen.

"What're you doing?" he called after her.

"These dishes aren't going to do themselves," she said, opening the ancient dishwasher.

"You need to get back to the store," he said.

"In a minute," she promised.

After loading and switching on the dishwasher, Scotlyn took a few minutes to wipe down the countertops, bag up the trash and take it out, straighten up the living room, and start a load of laundry.

"Don't you try to put that laundry in the dryer," she said, bringing him a mug of coffee, black and strong, the way he liked it. "I'll be back later to do that."

"I ain't a kid," he said.

"Right," she said, putting on her coat. "I'll give this place a better cleaning on Sunday."

"You don't have to do that," he said, still looking at the television. Scotlyn took his empty to-go containers and put them in the trash. She knew that was his way of thanking her, and she patted his shoulder before leaving.

"I'll see you later," she said. Before closing the door behind her, she heard him say, "All right. Love you."

"Love you, too," she said.

Scotlyn couldn't help smiling as she drove back to the store. Her father always overdid it when it came to watching out for her, and expected her to overdo it when looking after the store, but he always refused any offer she made of taking care of him. If his back hadn't been hurting so bad, she knew he would've stopped her from doing what little cleaning she'd done. She sighed, putting her head on her hand, and her elbow on the door, wishing, once again, that he'd agree to see a doctor, but knowing his stubbornness wouldn't let him. She bit her lower lip, still thinking, worrying, and wondering if his back trouble could be a sign of something more, something that could've been taken care of years ago but not now. Things like that happened to people all the time. They'd go to the doctor with a small, miniscule complaint and the next thing you know, it's cancer or something.

Scotlyn grimaced as she steered her car back into town, kept grimacing until she passed by an open garage with a sign that read McIntyre Automotive in red lettering above it. Her eyes moved to a young dark-haired man standing in front, his back to the road, cell phone at his ear.

She didn't stop, but could feel her grimace break into a smile as she pushed her car past.

Chapter 5

I just don't know," Tommy said into the phone, rubbing a cloth along his favorite pistol. It already gleamed, with nary a scratch on it. It had been through every robbery with him, every one, and he, too, always escaped without even a bruise. It was his good luck charm, you might say.

Yes, he thought to himself. People underestimated a good gun.

When he got out of here and got the money out of this deal with James, he might leave this house and this town, but this gun was going with him.

"You sure she's all that interested in you if she put

the date off a whole day?" he continued. "I thought you said she had *quite* a thing for you."

"I told you," Jimmy said from the other end. "She said she had plans. We're still on for tonight."

"Jeff said she just went to Redford's with some other gal," Tommy countered, holding up the gun now and looking through the barrel. "Doesn't sound like very big plans to me."

"Well, you know what? I don't care what it sounds like to you," James said. His voice was calm, trained from years of dealing with hustlers who were far worse than Tommy, but now he could feel his free hand making a fist. He curled it under his other arm, closed his eyes, and breathed in. *Calm*, he thought to himself. "Trust me, I know this girl," he said, taking advantage of Tommy's silence on the other end now, trying to smooth this out. "You don't have a thing to worry about."

Tommy could feel his own hand tightening on the gun. "I hope not, Jimmy," he said, and hung up.

James stood with the phone to his ear, listening to no one on the other end for a long time before closing it and returning it to his pocket.

ೞೕೞ

The rest of Scotlyn's day passed slowly, until, of course, about a quarter 'til six when she'd just grabbed her makeup bag and was about to go freshen up as a couple of older ladies, probably around eighty or so, walked in with another lady that Scotlyn presumed to be one's daughter because she was younger, probably in her fifties. She was short and round, with permanent frown lines between her eyes and around her mouth. She walked slowly behind the two older women, not bothering to help them along, instead shoving her hands in her pockets and appraising every inch of the bookstore around her. She never looked directly at Scotlyn, even when Scotlyn greeted the three of them. Scotlyn could immediately feel an uneasiness arise in her shoulders as she put her makeup bag away.

She tried to smile and be polite and patient as the two older women questioned her on every single cookbook on the shelf. Scotlyn answered as thoroughly as she could, in the hopes that that would deter more questions, but it only created more, and the minutes ticked by at a faster rate.

Finally, at about six-fifteen, Scotlyn said, "Excuse me for a moment," and went and turned the "Closed" sign in the window, hoping they'd get the message, but they didn't. They just continued to compare the two books they'd narrowed it down to in the thirty minutes they'd been in there.

Scotlyn, feeling like she was about to explode, said in as sweet a voice as she could muster with clenched teeth, "Well, you could get both and then bring one back if it doesn't work."

"Oh, no," the fifties woman said almost before Scotlyn had stopped speaking. "I don't want to have to make another trip into town."

She'd been flipping through the latest copy of *People,* tossed it onto one of the armchairs instead of replacing it, and folded her meaty arms across her chest.

Scotlyn could feel almost every muscle tense, including her throat. She really felt like she was about to start crying. By six twenty-five, the women finally made up their minds and walked behind Scotlyn at a snail's pace to the register, while she tried not to hurry and keep from giggling hysterically as they took ten years to find the right credit card with which to pay. The women left just in time for James to hold the door open for them.

Well, Scotlyn conceded. *He saw me without much makeup yesterday.*

James smiled at the women. "Have a good evening," he said as they passed by him.

Only one thanked him. Scotlyn observed that, like her, he had opted for jeans. He'd also chosen a black button-up shirt and white T-shirt underneath, tucked into jeans, and was wearing a set of glasses with thin frames this time, though they complimented his looks more than they took away from them.

"Hey," he said, removing the glasses.

"Hey," she said. "I didn't know you wore glasses."

"Only at night when I'm driving," he said.

"Well," she said, hoping her voice wasn't shaky. "I

just have a few things to finish up and I'll be ready."

"Okay," he said, nodding easily. "Should I wait outside?"

"Oh no, it's fine," she said, gesturing to the armchairs as she retrieved the copy of *People* and replaced it.

Instead, he wandered to the periodicals and began flipping through a copy of *Time* while she counted down the register, trying not to glance up at him so much, missing her place a couple of times, and having to start over. When she finally finished, she entered it into the spreadsheet her dad kept of how much money they made each day and took note that they had done a few dollars more than the same day as last year and the day before. She made a note to tell him that as she zipped the money into the bank envelope.

"I'll be right back," she said and he looked up from his magazine and grinned briefly.

Her legs felt a bit unsteady as she walked to the back office but, as she locked the money in the safe, she started to feel strangely calm, like there wasn't a thing in the world to be nervous about. She freshened up her powder and applied a little lip gloss, trying not to overdo it, and by the time she closed and locked the back, she felt the rest of the nervousness fade, like most of the minutes in her life had been leading up to this one and she was ready. She rounded the corner and found him looking out the front window, at the lampposts shining

dimly, the crepe myrtles twinkling with tiny Christmas
lights that stayed on year-round, and the courthouse
illuminated by lights shining up at it from the ground.
Scotlyn hit the light switch under the counter, leaving the
little green Tiffany lamp on the counter lit, but James
didn't move. Quietly, she moved to stand beside him and
look at the scene, too.

"I'd forgotten how pretty this town is, lit up at
night," he said.

"Hmm," she said, taking in the scene, trying to see
the beauty a stranger saw in it.

He looked a moment longer before turning to her and
saying, "So, what's good to eat around here? I'm
starving."

She told him about Roman's, her favorite Greek-
Italian place, knowing it was like a date place, not
knowing if this actually was a date, but not wanting to eat
fast food again.

"Roman's," he repeated. "Italian?"

"Yeah," she said, and then thought, *uh-oh*. Maybe he
didn't like Italian food. "Is that all right? Do you like
Italian?"

"Only just about every day," he said.

"Good," she said, walking out first and holding the
door for him. She locked up behind them and led him to
the restaurant, which was just down the way. He made a
move to walk along the outer side of the sidewalk, gently
pushing her inward, a move that both charmed her and

made her feel protected, even in the smallest sense. She smiled, but didn't look at him as she did.

Roman's was in an older building on the square, though it was not an old restaurant, itself. There were hardwood floors on the inside that you couldn't walk across without making echoes that bounced off the walls of the cavernous room. An open kitchen was straight across the back, beyond the booths and tables that were sprinkled, not too closely together, throughout. The tables were strategically placed so that a large circular dance floor, which no one was taking advantage of, was in the middle of the room. Paintings by various local artists, done in all kinds of styles and colors, hung on the white walls.

A young teenage girl seated them at a table near the front window, handed them two leather-bound menus, and told them about a couple of specials. She smiled at both of them, but the smile lingered on James for a few seconds before she turned away. Scotlyn smiled to herself, half-wondering if the girl would have lingered and bothered with stating the specials had it just been Scotlyn dining, or Scotlyn and Jane. Her suspicions were confirmed when she saw the girl seat two older women at a corner booth and immediately walk away.

"This is nice," he said, holding up the candle that was wedged into a green incandescent wine bottle, unaware of the girl watching him.

Scotlyn laughed.

"What?" he asked, replacing the candle.

"That girl was totally checking you out," she said in a low voice, not wanting the girl to hear.

"No," he said, looking up and around, then back at Scotlyn. "Seriously?"

Scotlyn laughed again at his obliviousness. But, she had to admit, that was part of his charm. Their waiter, another teenager, though a guy this time who reminded Scotlyn of James as a teenager, came over and set a basket of French bread in front of them and took their drink orders.

"It has been so long since I've had sweet tea," James said, sitting back and looking at the menu.

Scotlyn was about to say something back when they heard some heavy footsteps behind them and both turned in time to see Jonathan Smith reach their table, his eyes on James.

"I thought that was you," Jonathan said, still looking at James. "I had to come over and say hi."

James raised his eyebrows, obviously not recognizing Jonathan, who was still grinning like an idiot. Scotlyn remembered how "cool" Jonathan had been in school, how he had piercings up his ears and wore his brown hair long on top, but in a ponytail to show off how he'd shaved it underneath, skater style. Now, he was the typical family man: khaki's, loafers, button-up shirt, and hair short all over. He'd bought a big house on West Main and had gone to work as a loan officer.

"You're James McIntyre, right?" he said, still not acknowledging Scotlyn, though she was looking up at him.

She folded her arms over the table and pretended to study her menu.

"Jonathan Smith," he said, putting his palm over his chest. "You played soccer the '01 season at Laurel Springs High. I did, too."

Scotlyn rolled her eyes and then cut them to James, who gave her a hint of a smile before turning his attention to Jonathan.

"Oh, Jonathan," James said and reached out to shake his hand. "Yeah, I remember you." He gestured at Scotlyn. "I don't know if you remember Scotlyn Cart—"

"Oh. Right. Hey," Jonathan said before immediately turning his attention back to his idol. "I just wanted to tell you that the season you played was the only season we made it to state, and it was all because of you, man. You saved our team."

James laughed easily, shaking his head. "You're very kind."

"Really," Jonathan said. Scotlyn half wondered if he was just going to pull up a chair.

"Well," James said after a second. "Thanks."

"Yeah, no problem."

James continued to nod at Jonathan with a blank smile on his face and she had to cover her mouth with the back of her hand to keep from laughing.

"Well, it's good to see you," James finally said. "Thanks for coming by."

"Yeah, you too," Jonathan said, clearly not taking the hint. "So, are you back in town?"

James told him about helping his father re-open the garage, cutting his eyes to Scotlyn every few seconds and finally winking at her, making her smile. A few endless moments later, Jonathan returned to his family on the other side of the restaurant, leaving them alone, but not before patting Scotlyn on the arm and saying, "Sorry for interrupting your dinner, miss."

"Not at all," Scotlyn said, looking out the window instead of at him. A man stopped at one of the benches in front of the courthouse and sat facing them, though he didn't seem to be watching them. She couldn't tell. James's eyes followed hers and landed on the man. His expression stilled for a second before turning back to her, almost forcefully, and saying, "Sorry about that."

"You know him?" she asked.

"Who, Jonathan? No, can't say that I actually remembered him. Hated to lie, but—you know."

"No, the guy on the bench," she said, nodding her head toward the man.

"No, just wondering why someone's just sitting there alone at night like that." He looked at the man a second longer before turning back to her. "So, what's good to eat here?"

Scotlyn told him what she liked best, the spaghetti,

and that it was as good as any he'd get anywhere, and he ordered it without looking at the rest of the menu. When the waiter took their menus, Scotlyn sat back and looked at him. "Think I know now how Hugh Grant's character felt in *Notting Hill*."

The reference was lost on James. "What?"

"*Notting Hill* is a movie. Hugh Grant is this average, everyday guy who goes out with this superstar actress, and he has to deal with that—"

James ran his hands over the back of his head and rested them there. "I'm far from a superstar," he said.

Scotlyn shrugged but thought, *Not around here*. She didn't push it, though, seeing as how he didn't want to talk about it, a truth he voiced when he said, "I don't really want to talk about that. Tell me about where all you went after high school. You said you did some traveling."

"Well, it's not as fabulous as it sounds," she said. "I drove out to the Grand Canyon after college, stopping at a few places along the way."

She told him about stopping in New Orleans, Texas, and Las Vegas before settling in Arizona for a couple of years. She told him about how she felt like a stranger everywhere she went, but how that was okay because she'd always felt like a stranger, even in her hometown because not many people could relate to her and she couldn't to relate them. At least traveling from place to place allowed her to be the new person for a while, to be someone else if she wanted, and she'd tried that, though she had found it all but exhausting, so she'd moved again. She'd found a second home in Arizona. The town she'd settled in was quiet, and from her tiny house she could see nothing but the deep reds and browns of the mountainous desert that would turn a brilliant orange at sunrise.

"I could've stayed there forever," she admitted, there in that tiny house making just enough to get by as a waitress, but still happy because she was living in a place she loved.

"Why didn't you?" he asked, though the question was not disrespectful. As he looked at her, she could see that he just really wanted to know about her time, and her.

Scotlyn shrugged. "My dad—I couldn't say 'no' when he called me up, asked me to come home."

"Oh, right. Is he sick?" James asked, taking a drink of his tea.

"No," Scotlyn said then reconsidered. "Well, he has a lot of back pain, though he refuses to see a doctor. I'm just about the only person in the world who can help."

James leaned forward in his chair, pushed a salt shaker forward a few inches. "Your mom?" he asked.

"Gone," Scotlyn said. "Since I was a baby."

"Gone?" James repeated.

Scotlyn told him about her mother, her liveliness, how she and Scotlyn's father had married so young, and that her mother had just up and left, getting the travel bug the way Scotlyn had. "I think in some ways I was looking for her when I traveled," Scotlyn said, admitting that out loud for the first time, but then she shrugged as if it were nothing. "But I don't know. You know she never even filed for divorce? We don't know where she is to this day—probably on a beach somewhere. Dad said she loved the beach."

She looked back at James and he half smiled, hearing the sadness in her tone.

"You look like her?" he asked.

Scotlyn reached into her purse and pulled out the only other possession she had to remind her of her mother. It was a picture of her holding Scotlyn as a baby. She handed it to him. He looked at the picture, though he didn't smile and didn't look back at Scotlyn. When he finally handed it back, he said, "Beautiful. You do look like her."

Scotlyn looked back, feeling her heart in her chest. "You're kind."

She replaced the picture. She knew every inch of it by heart, could draw it without looking at it. Even now, she could see in her mind's eye her mother's long, dark hair, slight figure, and angular cheekbones she'd inherited.

And she could see the spirit in her mother's smile, the spirit that Scotlyn hadn't gotten, a look that said the world wasn't going to be the same when she was done with it.

James shook his head. "You're actually very kind for coming back and helping your father."

"There was no question about it," she said. "Guess that's one of the things I hold dear. Family."

She told him a little of how her father was overprotective of her growing up and still was, despite her years, but how she didn't so much mind it anymore.

"It's amazing how we change when we get older," he said, taking a bite of the spaghetti that the waiter had just set in front of him. "This is good."

"You don't really seem to have changed."

He looked at her for a second before saying, in a low voice, "I have."

"Tell me," she said.

"Tell you what?"

"Tell me everything. Where you were, what you did. I want to know. I just told you a lot—"

Though not everything, she mused, thinking about the robbery, or after-robbery, rather, that she'd witnessed, and how she wasn't quite ready to tell him something that intense. *Maybe if we get closer.*

"All right, let's see," he said, obviously trying to pick out some of the highlights of his life. "When I left here, I went back to Montana to my uncle's ranch. I mainly helped him with the new horses, breaking them in, training, things like that. Did that for probably three years until I broke my leg in two places, my arm, some ribs, my collarbone, punctured a lung and...oh yeah, ruptured my spleen, too." He pointed at each part he'd just cataloged, which was a lot.

Scotlyn's mouth was already open when she said, "All at once?"

She waited for him to tell her he was kidding. But instead he shrugged.

"It was a red stallion. He threw me...well, it isn't that uncommon, especially when you train them. Especially stallions. I'd been thrown before, but never fell that hard. It was the trampling that really did the damage, though."

"Trampling?" she repeated.

"Yeah," James said without missing a beat. "He threw me into a fence and then trampled over me when he jumped it."

Scotlyn brought her hand to her mouth. She'd never known he'd been through all that. "Oh, my." She couldn't help but wonder where she was and what she was doing the minute that happened to him.

He moved his shoulder around a bit. "I survived it. When I finally did get out of the hospital, doc said I wouldn't ride again. Proved him wrong on that, though." James pointed his fork at Scotlyn, making her smile, before continuing with his story. "Anyway, I tried to get back to work, but I just couldn't ...I don't know. Something changed. I couldn't really do as good at work as I did before, and it was all I'd ever done, so, naturally I was a little lost."

He stopped to take a drink of his tea, stared out the window for a moment. "But I was still strong, could do some heavy lifting and things, so my uncle hooked me up with this construction crew he knew needed a hand, and that was that, I guess."

Scotlyn listened, taking a bite but not really tasting the food. She listened to his stories of how he, too, had traveled from place to place, working on different construction sites, but never really taking in the place, just mainly traveling for the work.

"You ever miss working with horses?" she asked, looking at his eyes. She could've looked at his eyes all evening. She brought a hand to her mouth and bit down slightly on one of her nails.

"Sometimes." Then he looked up. "But that chapter's closed. And I made some pretty good friends, traveling."

He took a final bite and brought his tea to his mouth again.

Scotlyn decided to move forward with another question that had been on her mind. "Girlfriends?"

He held his glass there for a second, looking only at her. He didn't seem angered by the question or scared off, only thinking about how to answer it, but his pausing showed her he didn't have to. Finally, he just smiled and set his glass on the table. That was enough of an answer for Scotlyn.

She did feel a twinge of jealousy, but knew she shouldn't. It had been almost fifteen years since they'd seen one another, and they'd not so much as touched, let alone dated.

"You?" he asked.

"Did I have girlfriends?" she asked, and he winked at her again. "No," she continued, smiling. "There were a few guys. Justin," she began, and told him about that boyfriend in Arizona that she left growing smaller and more bewildered in the background as she drove home to her father. "And Raylan," she said. "He was cool, not in a good way, unsympathetic."

She let that be the end of it. She didn't want them to share too much of their romantic pasts. It wasn't right. If they let the ghosts of past relationships sit at their table, then it wouldn't just be the two of them anymore.

And right now, all Scotlyn wanted was for it to be just them.

"It *is* fun, though, isn't it?" he asked. She looked at him. "Traveling," he clarified.

"Oh, yeah," she said. "It is."

"Sometimes a little lonely," he said, looking out the window.

She looked his way again, but didn't say anything right away. He was right, it was. Moving around, not knowing anyone. It could get lonely. She suddenly felt happy to be in the presence of someone who understood that. Both Jane and Scotlyn's father had thought it a little strange that Scotlyn had wanted to just up and travel around by herself, with no one. No one really understood, her need to do so and how it felt when she did—until now.

"Yeah," she said, nodding slowly.

She pushed her plate away and they sat in silence for a while, enjoying the company of each other.

A fast song finished in the speakers overhead and then a slower one, one Scotlyn remembered from a long time ago, started. It was a woman singing to someone about how she yearned to be that certain someone's lover. It had a slow, yet steady beat, but a longing to it that matched the lyrics. Scotlyn looked at the dance floor. A few couples had started to dance.

"You dance?" James asked, bringing her back to him.

Scotlyn turned. *Oh, no.* "Not really," she admitted, not wanting to show off her lack of coordination. At the same time, though, she wanted him to convince her to dance with him.

He stood up, offering his hand. "Neither do I."

But I bet you'll be good at it, she thought, looking at his eyes a moment before giving in and taking his hand.

He led her to the floor and easily pulled her to him, holding the small of her back with one hand and lightly holding her hand to his shoulder with the other. Scotlyn hesitantly put her other hand on his arm. She could feel her cheeks burn and everything in her tremble as he moved her, guiding her with his legs, not worried about whether others were looking. She looked down or off to the side, conscious of the warmth from him until she could feel the steady beat and rhythm of the song move into her chest, relaxing her. She closed her eyes, let him lead her, until he turned her and she went with it easily. He didn't bring her around to face him, though, brought her shoulders into his chest instead, resting his arms over hers as they kept moving to the song, just letting it be their guide. He turned her to face him again, and their eyes didn't leave one another's until the song ended and they stopped, the spell broken.

"Liar," he said.

"What?" she asked.

"You dance well."

She shrugged. "Well—"

"I'm sorry," he said, and she looked at him.

"For what?"

He leaned in at that moment and kissed her in front of everyone. If others were looking, Scotlyn didn't notice. She noticed nothing but the warmth of his lips against hers.

"For that," he said after he pulled away, his face still close.

Scotlyn's heart had picked up again, though she didn't want her inhaler to stop it. She just smiled. "Don't you dare be sorry."

Chapter 6

Scotlyn couldn't pull the smile from her face all night, even after James had walked her back to her car, after she'd gone to finish her dad's laundry, after she got into bed, completely unafraid for the first time in a long time. James had not kissed her good-night before closing her driver's side door for her, letting his hand linger on the window for a moment, but Scotlyn wasn't disappointed. They'd stayed in the restaurant for a long time after, still dancing slowly, even when a more upbeat song came on. Eventually, the owner had to kick them out.

Scotlyn replayed the night and the dance in her mind,

even now, as she stood at the counter at the bookstore, trying to focus on the catalog of books her dad asked her to look through to make recommendations for orders. She'd probably skipped over half a dozen titles the store could've used, and would have to look those pages over again later. She didn't really mind, though. As with a lot of things, she didn't mind extra work when she was still floating and drifting the day after a romantic encounter.

About an hour into her day, the phone rang and, before Scotlyn got the telephone greeting out of her mouth, Jane said, "I want details."

Scotlyn halfway rolled her eyes but still smiled to herself, admittedly eager to tell her friend about the date.

"He actually kissed you?" Jane practically screamed after shrieking like a teenager.

Scotlyn couldn't help but shake her head at how someone like Jane, who'd experienced the bad side of love first hand, could still have such an idealized, excited view of romance.

"So, tell me more," she said when she recovered.

"I don't think there's really anything else to tell."

"Are you going out again?"

"We sort of made plans, but not really."

"Well," Jane said. "I think he's definitely calling you. He's got to be smitten."

"No, you're talking about me, thanks in part to you. Guys are different, remember? If he wants to go out with me again, I won't even notice until he asks me."

"Whatever," Jane said. "I still think he'll call."

"Well, you can hold your breath for both of us," Scotlyn said, and looked up as a couple of men came into the store and walked right up to the counter, waiting silently for her to finish her conversation.

"I'd better go," she said, nodding once to the men and smiling to let them know she wasn't ignoring them.

"Okay," Jane said. Then, "Wait, what do you mean, 'thanks' to me?"

"Figure it out," Scotlyn said before hanging up and turning to the men.

She really wished Jane hadn't done that. Now she was going to get her hopes up again and, despite her euphoria, had been trying to keep her head level. She tried to concentrate on helping the two men select the best book she had on tree surgery, and then spent the rest of the day tirelessly dusting counters, rearranging displays on tables, and combing through the catalog with unparalleled concentration.

That didn't stop her from jumping when the phone rang, though it was never James on the other end. It was always someone wanting to know where they were located, if they had any copies of a certain book, or how late they were open. When she returned the catalog to her father at the end of the day, she was almost angry, though she didn't know if it was at herself, Jane, or James. Her dad took the catalog from her and looked over the selections, his reading glasses propped on his nose. When he noticed his daughter hovering, he looked up. "Everything all right?"

Scotlyn looked at him, almost startled. She hadn't realized she'd been pausing for so long. "Oh yeah," she said, trying to wave it off, though she never could fool him.

He could've pressed the issue, but instead he tugged at the collar of his navy long-sleeved polo shirt and told her she could take the rest of the day off if she wanted. Scotlyn was tempted to say 'yes,' but then wondered what she'd do. Sit at home, just waiting on James to call?

Grow up, she commanded. *You're not in high school anymore.*

"Okay, I'll go home," she said. She left the bookstore, got into her car, and began the drive home, where she planned to get ready for a long, long run.

෧෨෧

Scotlyn slowed her pace as she could feel blood in her throat and her chest caving. She'd overdone it for sure this time. She slowed to a walk, satisfied with the four miles she'd done that night. She'd come to the high school track this time, not wanting to risk her dad seeing her running around town again and getting another lecture.

She stretched out her arms as she walked the last lap around the track. The sky was already dark enough for the track lights to come on, brightly illuminating the dark pathway and the soccer field it encircled. There was only one other man on the track at that hour, a tall, muscled man with long brown hair that flopped around as he jogged. A runner for years now, Scotlyn couldn't help but notice how his pace was uneven, picking up and slowing every few steps.

She tried not to stare, remembering how she'd once been a novice, too, before her track days in high school, but she couldn't help it.

Finally, she realized it wasn't just his uneven pace, but something else, in his build, in the way he carried himself that made her keep looking his way.

As she rounded the last turn, she couldn't help but take her phone out of her pocket and check it, just be sure James hadn't called. He hadn't.

She cursed under her breath as she replaced the cellular in her pocket.

"Something wrong?" came a voice from behind her and Scotlyn jumped, turning and finding the greasy-haired man walking a few steps behind her, smiling, revealing jagged teeth. Scotlyn could feel her shoulders tense and wondered for a second if she could outrun him to her car.

"Uh, no," she said, trying to smile back, trying to be polite but still find a way to get out of there quickly. She turned back, continuing her walk, but he walked up closer beside her.

"You run good," he said, now even closer.

"Thanks," she said, looking straight ahead.

"Just started, myself," he said. "Trying to work out more. New Year's Resolution, you know?"

"Yeah," Scotlyn said. *Get away.* She made a move to start walking up the grassy knoll to the parking lot. "Well, see you," she said, not turning.

"Yeah, see you, Scotland," he said, sending a bolt of lightning through her chest.

She turned, waiting for an explanation.

"I came into your bookstore," he said, saying the word "your" as if he were tasting it. "A while back."

She studied him, frozen. What was happening here? Who remembered employees from random stores, except creepy, crooked-toothed scoundrels who had less than honorable intentions? "Oh. Sorry, I don't remember you."

"Ah," he said, waving that away. "I didn't buy anything. But I saw you there, sitting behind the counter. Heard some man call to you from the back. Was that your daddy?"

"Uh, yeah, yeah it was," she said, nodding, now backing her way toward her car and searching her pockets for her keys.

"You look really good, Scotland," he said, continuing to walk toward her. "I like that name, by the way. Scotland. Hadn't heard it before. You named after the country, or what?"

She didn't like the way he used it. "It's Scot*lyn*,

actually," she said, digging ferociously in her pockets now, mentally cursing.

"Oh, excuse *me*," he said, holding up his hands as if to surrender, still smiling.

She found her keys but immediately dropped them. Before she could reach down to get them, he grabbed them and playfully dangled them just out of her reach.

Oh, no.

"You dropped these," he said.

No kidding, she thought, but tried to smile and reached toward them. Just before her hand reached them, he yanked them away, laughing. Scotlyn tried to laugh, though she could feel her throat closing.

Finally, he handed them to her and she took them with two fingers.

"You'd better be careful, Scot*lyn*," he said.

Scotlyn swallowed hard and focused on nodding and keeping the smile on her face, trying to force the moment to stay lighter than it was. "Well, good-bye," she said.

"Yeah," he said. "Hope to see you again soon."

Scotlyn closed and locked the door to her Civic, started it, put it in gear, and slammed the accelerator. She could see him still smiling after her in her rearview mirror.

એજી

"Hello?"

"James?"

He sat up in his bed, phone to his ear, and glanced at the digital clock on his nightstand: 7:46. Damn, how had he slept so long? "Scotlyn?" he said, rubbing his eyes with the back of his hand. She sounded scared, shaky. "What's wrong?" he continued. "Where are you?"

"Uh, I'm at home," she said, obviously trying to sound casual, like she was making too big a deal out of something.

Don't think that, he ordered silently. *Tell me.*

"It was probably nothing," she said. "I just—there was this guy—"

"Wait," he said, getting out of bed. *Tread lightly*, he reminded himself. "Have you eaten dinner yet?" he asked.

"Um, no," she said.

"Do you want to meet somewhere?" he asked. "Or…" *If you're too scared, I could come over.* The words were probably a bit too much to say to her at this point in their relationship. *Relationship?* "Or do you just want to talk on the phone?"

Scotlyn paused. "I don't know."

Whatever had happened, she didn't want to be alone. He could tell. "I can come get you," he offered. "We could go somewhere, if you want, or just drive around."

"Okay," Scotlyn agreed.

"Where do you live?" he asked. Scotlyn told him. "I'll be there in twenty minutes," he said and hung up.

∽◌∽

Scotlyn showered as quickly as she could, closing and locking the bathroom door and then easing it open with painful slowness when she got out.

Everything's fine, she told herself, but still hurried back to her room. She pulled on jeans and a pink long-sleeved T-shirt as fast as she could. When her back doorbell rang, she was perched on the edge of her bed, waiting, and jumped up before the buzzer even finished sounding. She grabbed her jacket and purse, double-checked the front door to make sure it was locked, and went to the back. She paused, pulling aside the fitted curtain over the window, to ensure that it was indeed James on the other side, and opened the door.

Before she even said "Hi" or got the door closed behind her, he enveloped her in a hug and she clung to him. She didn't cry, but she could feel the raggedness in her chest as she struggled to breathe.

"You all right?" he asked after he released her.

Scotlyn nodded. "I just didn't really want to be alone," she admitted as she closed and locked the door behind her.

Taking her by the hand, he led her to the black Charger that was parked in her gravel driveway. He turned left on to the road, though she hadn't told him where to go. She was grateful he hadn't asked, had just made a decision for her because she really was in no

mood or condition to be making decisions. They just
drove along the little two-lane road until they came to
Main Street, and he made a right. Overhead streetlights
streaked the inside of the car now and then, and Scotlyn
looked at the beautiful old homes they passed,
maintaining their original beauty. If it weren't for the cars
they occasionally passed, one might think they had
actually gone through a portal and arrived in the
nineteenth century.

"You hungry?" James finally asked.

Scotlyn thought about it. She hadn't had anything
since lunch and the run had worked up an appetite. But
the greasy-haired man had left her stomach tight and her
nerves so worked up that she'd probably have some
trouble swallowing anything.

"Maybe later," she said.

He didn't ask her what had happened, just gave her
some time and space. She'd felt a little stupid for just
calling him out of the blue, but she hadn't wanted to deal
with her father's overprotective questions and Jane's
hysterics if she'd told them. So she called the only other
person she'd wanted to talk to all day and when he
hugged her, he immediately put her at ease and chased
away all of the stupidity she'd felt for calling him in the
first place.

"These houses are so great," he said as they passed
them. It was obvious he wasn't going to push her if she
didn't want to talk about what had happened. He was just

going to be there, which was exactly what she needed.

She looked at him as he drove. "Something did happen tonight," she said. He waited. She swallowed. "I was out jogging—at the track at the high school—so my father wouldn't see." She laughed a little. "He gets kind of worried since I'm asthmatic."

She could see him smile a little and nod, still looking at the road ahead.

"There was someone else there, a man. He was kind of creepy, weird. Said he'd recognized me from being in the store a while back. I don't know, maybe it's nothing. Maybe I'm making too much out of this."

As she told James the story, it sounded far less creepy than when it had actually happened, and she suddenly felt stupid again. "I don't know," she said with a shake of her head. "It was just weird. *He* was weird, the way he looked at me, teased me."

She looked at him out of the corner of her eye to gauge his reaction, to see if maybe he thought she was making this up just to see him again. All she could see, or thought she could see, anyway, was him tighten his grip on the steering wheel.

"I don't know, it's stupid," she said. "I'm sorry I bothered you."

"You're not a bother," he said. "Actually, I was planning on calling *you* tonight. You just happened to beat me to the punch."

She half-laughed at his joking attempt. Should she

tell him about the robbery? That that was what was really making her jerky and jumpy and making her call a guy she'd only had one date with? Scotlyn waited, watching for his reaction.

It was probably too soon to tell him, she thought. She didn't want to scare him off by confiding too much information in him. That was something that would have to wait.

"You know something, I *am* a little hungry," she said.

He nodded once. "I was hoping you'd say that." He turned the car around, got them some burgers and fries from the drive-thru at the Clock, and then headed back toward the country. "I know where we can go."

Scotlyn settled back in her seat, not asking where they were going, content to let him take her wherever. They drove past the old houses once again, past the schools and churches and other places Scotlyn had grown up around until they were exiting what little civilization there was and entering the countryside.

James turned off the main road and drove a few miles before turning again into a wooded area. He drove along a narrow road, slowly, until it opened into a larger parking lot. The headlights from his car illuminated a hill just beyond that lowered to a dock over the darkness of a wide lake that seemed to go on for miles. Scotlyn could faintly make out trees surrounding the lake in the distance.

"Wow," she said, handing him one of the to-go boxes. "This is beautiful."

"Yeah, it's nice," he confirmed. "I was hoping you'd like it."

James reached into the console and pulled out a bottle of aspirin. Scotlyn watched as he popped two in his mouth and swallowed them without a drink. He caught sight of her watching and she could feel her cheeks burn as she became embarrassed for staring at him.

He rubbed his shoulder "Just hurts when it's about to rain."

"Oh," she said, remembering his broken bones. She felt a minor stab in her own. They didn't say anything for a few minutes, just ate in silence until Scotlyn thought about something.

"How did you know about this place?" she asked.

James shrugged good-naturedly. "My dad and I lived on this lake when we lived here when I was a kid. We used to fish here all the time."

"You're a fisherman?" she asked.

"Well, I wouldn't survive *Deadliest Catch*, but yeah, sometimes my dad and I would go."

Scotlyn laughed to herself. Then she thought about something else. James had never once mentioned his mother, even when they were teens, even after Scotlyn had told him the story of hers.

"Where's your mom?" she asked.

James chewed on a fry for a few seconds, looking at

the few raindrops that were beginning to fall on his windshield. "She died," he said finally, taking a drink from his Coke.

"Oh," she said, paralyzed. "I'm sorry."

She didn't know if she should go on with the conversation or just leave it, but he finished it for her.

"That's why my dad and I moved out here in the first place," he said, still looking forward. The rain was making a steady hum now as more drops fell at a faster rate. He took a bite of another fry. "It was cancer. We thought she had it beat, but when it came back, she was gone, just like that."

"Were you close?" Scotlyn asked.

James shrugged, tilting his head to the side once. "Not really. You know how most teens are with their parents. It was weird, even when she was in the hospital, sick, and they told us it was only a matter of time, I didn't believe it. It was like a part of me just kept thinking she'd get better and come home, you know?"

Scotlyn nodded, though she *didn't* know.

He laughed, though there was no humor in his voice. "You know, once, in fifth grade she wouldn't let me go to a friend's house, a guy—I don't even remember his name. Anyway, she said he was a bad influence and forbade me to go over there. I remember telling her I hated her and didn't speak to her for days after." He stared out the windshield at the rain that was now falling steadily, almost drowning out their voices. "It's weird the things you remember…" he said, his voice drifting away.

Scotlyn looked at his profile a long time. "You know she didn't believe you really hated her. I don't know if there's one parent out there who hasn't heard that at least once."

"I know," he said.

"I remember telling my dad that, once," she admitted. "I was around twelve, maybe thirteen. He wouldn't let me wear a mini-skirt to some girl's birthday party."

"Regrets…" James said, letting the thought hang in the air.

"You ever apologize?"

"Yeah," he said. "But it was, like, after she was gone, all of these other memories came to mind. I couldn't stop thinking about all the times I'd let her down or said other things that probably hurt her feelings."

"What was your best memory of her?" she said suddenly, remembering Dr. Brenner saying something similar to her, once, about her own mother.

He hesitated for a moment, looking at her. "The circus. I was ten. It was just me and her. My dad had to work or something. She would clap and cheer with me every time I got excited. We laughed a lot. I remember I loved the lions, told her I wanted one for a pet. And do you know what she did?"

Scotlyn shook her head.

"After it was over, she somehow found the lion

tamer, or whatever he was, and convinced him to let her bring me over to the lions' cages so I could get a closer look. Of course, I couldn't pet them, but..." His voice trailed off, his point made.

Scotlyn leaned in then and kissed him. It took him a moment, but finally he began to return it. They sat there all night that night, talking, sharing other bits from their individual lives, laughing, and finally dozing across from one another as the rain continued its steady hum throughout the night.

Chapter 7

The next morning when Scotlyn woke up, things weren't right—not just one thing—several things. Her neck was stiff and when she pushed the covers back, she saw she was still in her T-shirt and jeans, though her shoes lay with uncharacteristic neatness at the foot of her bed. Rolling rolled her neck around, she winced at the stab of a crick.

She shuddered and felt her breath catch in her chest then reached for her inhaler. She wrapped a blanket around herself to shut out the cold as she shuffled to the kitchen to make coffee.

But she didn't make it that far.

She didn't see him until she was almost out of the living room. She was so used to seeing piles of clothes all over the place, which at first glance, he seemed to blend in with them. He was sleeping until she screamed. He jolted upward, pulling one of her shirts off his face.

"James?" she said, still clutching the wall behind her. It took a few heavy breaths before she was assured that it was actually him.

He rubbed his eyes with the back of his hand. "Hey."

Then fragments of the previous night came back to her. Driving around with James, sharing pieces of their lives as they ate cheeseburgers in his car, talking and dozing until—that was it. She must have fallen asleep.

"Sorry," he said, stretching his arms out in front of him. "I didn't mean to scare you. I was sure I'd wake up before you."

"I don't sleep, at least not much," she admitted. *And so much scares me these days.*

He nodded, standing as he ran a hand through his long dark hair. "Well, I'll leave you to your morning routine."

He tried to smile, but was still too sleepy, she could see, to fully form the expression, so she said, "Here, at least let me make you some coffee."

She started a pot and, as they waited for it to brew, she asked, "How is it that you came to stay here?"

"We both fell asleep in my car," he said, looking out her bay windows, at the crystalline day around them. "I woke up about two, drove back here, put you to bed. I took off your shoes and you said 'Wait.'"

"Wait?" She'd always talked in her sleep, or at least she'd been told.

"Wait." He shrugged and apologized, told her he didn't mean to overstep boundaries, but didn't like the idea of leaving her alone, either.

She brought him his coffee. She hoped he liked it as strong as she liked hers. Her dad always told her that the coffee she made was so thick, one could eat it with a spoon. James didn't make a face, though, when he took a sip from the mug she placed before him. She sat across from him and drew a knee to her chest. For a long time they sat across from one another in silence, as if they did that every morning.

"I'm glad you stayed," she finally said.

He looked up at her, his green eyes a little brighter, a little more with her. He didn't say anything, but his expression told her what she needed to know—he was happy, too.

಄಄಄

James didn't wait until he got back home. In his car, he dialed the number he'd become grudgingly familiar with.

It rang three times before a voice answered on the other end.

"You want to tell me what the hell you were doing last night?"

Tommy chuckled. "Relax, Jimmy. We just thought she might need a little probing, that's all. Did it work? Did the little bunny come running to you and confess everything?"

"I told you *not* to interfere." James said the words slowly, ignoring the question.

"I wasn't. I was just taking a jog on a nice evening. You know? I almost forgot how hot she was."

"Don't even think about it."

Tommy laughed again. "Don't worry, Jimmy. I'll be sure and keep Jeff in his cage."

"Try locking yourself in, too."

Tommy laughed again in response.

James wanted to crush the phone in his hand. "Don't think I don't know who was watching us the other night, too," he said, pulling into his driveway.

"Ah, you know Clay won't do anything," Tommy said. "He just wanted to be sure you made direct contact. Said you two made a nice-looking couple, by the way. Pity you're just playing her, huh? Well, maybe it's not all for nothing. You'll probably at least get a few good lays out of this, right?"

"Don't forget, I'm doing you a favor, giving you the chance to work with the big guys and create a better life for yourselves. I see or hear of any of you lurking around again, this deal is off. Do you understand?"

Tommy sighed. There was no laughter or comedy to his tone now. He said the only thing he could say. "All right, Jimmy. If that's the way you want to play it."

James hung up the phone, got out of his car, and pushed his back door open. He tossed his jacket and keys on the table and went to the window over the kitchen sink, noticing, for the first time, that the fig tree outside had a lone fruit hanging low, almost to the ground.

He looked at it until his thoughts turned to Martin, and he couldn't help but wonder if he should just call the man up and have him speed up the deal with these three losers and let that be the end of it. Leave Scotlyn to the safety of her own life. He knew that was what he should do. Martin would take some convincing, but he'd come around eventually. Still…

James would never see Scotlyn again.

"Scotlyn," he said out loud and rubbed the back of his neck.

She's just another victim, he thought to himself, closing his eyes. *She'd be better off without you, without this danger.*

But she still liked him, he could see, and he knew how distraught she'd be if he just up and left the way he had when they were teenagers. It was true that he'd enjoyed the company of more than a few women over the past several years, but something about the way Scotlyn talked to him, the way she looked at him with her pretty eyes and shy smile, as if he was the only man on earth.

She understood, albeit in a different way, what it was like to lose a mother, to travel alone in this world, and to want to be alone but still be lonely.

James sighed. He knew that he didn't just want her protected. He wanted to be the one to protect her and be with her, probably indefinitely.

☙❦❧

The next morning Scotlyn smiled as she thanked the young, blonde barista at the coffee shop on the square, leaving her a good tip in the process. She grabbed her two cappuccinos and the bag containing one blueberry and one maple nut muffin and headed to the bookstore. The rain that had fallen all the previous night had left wet and damp patches on the sidewalk here and there, but today the sun shone brightly and it was warm—almost seventy degrees.

She could hear the call of some mourning doves on the wind, a call she had mistaken for owls when she was a kid. She took a long sip of her cappuccino, waving to the man in the Buick who let her cross in front of him, and jogged to the door of the bookstore.

She knew she should pace herself in her feelings for James, but something was starting to get beyond her control. The way he listened to her without judgment, without probing her with questions, letting her tell him however much she wanted at her own pace and then just talking, really talking, made her feel better than she had in a long time.

Before he left that morning, he invited her and her father to meet his own later that week, hence the muffins she was carrying. She was always nervous meeting new people, but thought it was nice that James had invited both her and her father over. With other people she knew, it would make everything more comfortable.

She knew she probably didn't need the muffins so much to convince her father, that he would probably be impressed enough that a young man had taken the initiative to have them both over, rather than just keep Scotlyn to himself.

She couldn't help but smile at the ideas that thought conjured as she pushed open the glass door of the bookstore.

"Hey, Dad," she said to the top of her father's head as he leaned over the figures from yesterday. He looked up and smiled. Scotlyn wasn't surprised. There were quite a few people in there today, at least one or two on every aisle.

"We've already done more money today than the same day last year," he said, pointing a pen in her direction.

"Wow," Scotlyn said, handing over one of the cappuccinos and the bag containing the muffins.

"What's this?" he asked. "You're giving business to the other coffee shop?"

Scotlyn waved him off. "I'm just treating you."

"You want to treat me? Stay loyal and buy coffee from your old man."

Despite the complaint, he still took a drink and looked at the cup after he did. "Not bad," he admitted, which was pretty much high praise, coming from him.

"I need a favor," she said, taking a sip of her own coffee.

"Ah," he said, rolling his eyes.

"You and I have been invited to dinner with a friend and his father."

"His?"

"Yes," she said. "You remember how I told you about James McIntyre?"

Her father didn't acknowledge it, but just let her go on.

"He said he wants us all to get together. He and his dad will cook for us at his dad's house."

"Hmm." Her father considered. "Well, I do have to say that this is a first."

"Might be fun," Scotlyn ventured.

"Ha!" he said, looked around his store then back at her. "All right, since it obviously means so much to you."

"Thanks," Scotlyn said, kissing him on the cheek as she passed by.

"Whatever, you need to get to work."

James called her later that evening, asking her what they wanted to eat later that week and she told him steak, knowing that that was her dad's favorite and that it would win him over almost immediately.

"Make sure you have plenty of sweet tea, too," she warned.

"Definitely," he answered. He gave her directions to the house, and told her to be there around seven on Tuesday.

*ↄ*ↄↄ*

"I don't see why we had to bring anything," her father asked as Scotlyn steered her car along Harper Street later that week toward James's father's house and their evening amongst strangers. He tugged at the collar of the tan button-up shirt she'd convinced him to wear. "They're the ones who invited *us*, remember?"

"It's polite and customary to bring a little something to your host's house," Scotlyn said, straining to see the numbers on the houses so she didn't miss it. She'd tried to persuade her father to bring a bottle of red wine, but he'd countered with, "I don't drink wine," and Scotlyn had ended up buying it herself at a liquor store in town just minutes ago. She made her father hold it.

"Okay, I think this is it," she said, slowing her car as they approached a two-story white house mainly obscured by two enormous magnolia trees out front. Scotlyn eased the car into the narrow gravel drive. It wasn't easy, considering stone walls flanked the drive and one wrong movement an inch in any direction would put a scratch on her car. The driveway was long, leading all the way to the back of the house, and at least two acres stretched beyond that. There was a wraparound porch with porch swings on both sides of the front door and a few rosebushes in the small yard. It was an old house, no doubt, but in good shape.

Inherited? Scotlyn wondered as she and her father shut their respective car doors and began walking toward the steps leading up to the back door.

"Damn, how many steps are there?" her father asked, holding onto the railing.

"Shhh!" Scotlyn said, waving him down. She rang the buzzer and almost immediately heard footsteps falling toward them. A minute later, James opened the door and smiled at Scotlyn, greeting them with, "Hey there, come on in."

Scotlyn and her father entered a long enclosed back porch that had windows stretching across it and housed a couple of large freezers. A doorway led into a bright kitchen with a small breakfast nook overlooking the rosebushes through bay windows. The modern day appliances seemed almost out of place in a kitchen that clearly was built before the rise of technological advancements.

"Thanks," James said, as Scotlyn's dad handed over the bottle of wine. "I'm James McIntyre."

"George Carter." Scotlyn's father introduced himself

as they shook hands, and Scotlyn felt herself relax a little.

James set the bottle of wine on the breakfast table. "Come on, I'll show you around."

He showed them the dining room that housed a long black table with a candelabra in the center and chairs around it with red velvet cushions that matched the carpet; the high-ceilinged, cavernous living room that seemed too big for even the two sofas; an antique roll-top desk in one corner; and a small television set in the other. Their footsteps made echoing sounds as they walked a long hallway toward the parlor near the front of the house. Scotlyn had seen pictures of places like this in magazines, in movies set in the old south—dainty, elegant end tables; pristinely cushioned sofas and chairs; fireplaces with detailed carvings on mantles that housed delicate porcelain figurines; candleholders that had actual prisms dangling from them; porcelain Chinese lamps.

"This is such a great house," she said, when he finished the tour.

"It belonged to my dad's grandmother," James said, confirming Scotlyn's suspicions. "She died about fifteen years ago and my great aunt lived here with her daughter until she passed away. Then her daughter decided to move back to Myrtle Beach a few months ago, and my dad said he'd just take the house rather than have her sell it. I was glad. I didn't want to see it go."

"You must have some good memories here," George said.

"Yeah, we used to come here for Christmas a lot, would spend up to two weeks here, sometimes. I used to get in trouble for running up and down the porch with my cousins. We were so loud that you could hear the echoes from our footsteps for miles."

"Boys will be boys," George said, looking at a couple of large, window-sized paintings that hung from wires extending clear from the ceiling. "So, your dad is starting up his garage again, right?" he asked.

"That's right," James nodded and pointed in the direction of the garage. "Up past where the old Greystone restaurant is."

Scotlyn watched James as he and her father talked about the new garage and everything else James had been up to the last several years. James answered her father's questions with slow, easy smiles, never revealing a hint of nervousness, if he even had any. He tucked his hands in his pockets, nodding as her father talked, like he was just talking with an old friend.

I think I'm in trouble, she thought as she took in the sight of him.

"Sorry my dad's not here yet," James said. "He went to get some butter and sour cream for the potatoes. Said there was no way we could eat them without all of that."

"No problem," George said. "Can you tell me where the john is?"

"Dad," Scotlyn said, shaking her head.

He looked at her. "*Bathroom*, all right?"

She rolled her eyes.

"Yeah, it's near the back of the house, just off the room that's past the living room."

"Got it," he said. "Don't you two get into trouble."

Scotlyn shook her head again and turned to look at a large mirror above one of the mantles.

As soon as her father was out of the room, though, she could feel James's hand move over her shoulder and to her neck before he kissed her, quickly at first, but lingering.

Scotlyn was taken aback, but went with it, reaching up to put her arms around him.

"Hey," he said when he released her.

"Hey, yourself," she said.

They heard the back door open just then, and both instinctively pulled apart, laughing a little as they realized how much like teenagers they were acting.

"James!" a gruff, but quiet voice called from the kitchen area.

"Coming!" James said, taking Scotlyn by the hand and leading her back to the kitchen.

When they got to the kitchen, Scotlyn saw James's twin standing over two brown grocery bags, unloading them. After a minute, though, the differences sank in— the graying hair at the temples, the slight hunch in the shoulders, the rougher hands that seemed to be permanently dark from working on cars.

"Dad, this is Scotlyn," James said, pulling her close

to his side. "Scotlyn Carter. Scotlyn, this is my dad, Sam."

Sam looked at her with weathered brown eyes, smiled, and offered his hand, which she took.

"Ms. Carter," he said. Scotlyn's dad appeared in the doorway of the kitchen, then, and the two men got a look at each other. "Hell," James's father said. "George Carter!"

"Sam McIntyre," Scotlyn's father said. "I knew I recognized your name!"

The men shook hands ferociously, clapping each other on the back, and going into how it had been so long since they'd seen one another, how they'd been, and what they had been up to.

James leaned in close and whispered to Scotlyn, "I think we could sneak away and they'd never even notice."

She playfully slapped his shoulder.

"Can't believe our kids are dating now," Scotlyn's father said with a laugh, patting her forearm.

"Dad," Scotlyn said warningly, and James looked at her while the two men continued their conversation as if their children weren't even in the room.

"We're not?" James asked in a playfully hurt tone.

Scotlyn looked at him, feeling a zigzag of emotions running up and down her chest and stomach.

Before she could respond, he leaned in and kissed her forehead.

"Well, come on, let's eat. I'm sure we're all starved," Sam said.

"Oh, isn't there anything we can do to help?" Scotlyn offered.

"Nope, everything's done," Sam said, patting her on the back. "Just have a seat."

They sat a little cramped at the breakfast nook, rather than the dining room, but it was still warm and cozy, and Scotlyn was grateful.

The dining room, she felt, would probably have seemed a little too formal.

"I hope you both like your steaks medium," Sam said, and Scotlyn and her father both said that was fine.

When he saw that Scotlyn was taking her potato plain, he took a spoonful of butter that could've fit into a bowl and dumped it on her potato.

"Oh," she said, sitting back. Before she could say anything further, he took a spoonful sour cream and dumped it on the potato, too.

"You have to eat it my way when you're at my house," he said, winking at her, but she still had the thought that she'd better do what he said.

Sam questioned Scotlyn on what she'd done since high school and how she liked working for her father. Scotlyn was a little nervous at first, but quickly found herself at ease.

James's father was good-natured, a man who'd spent years doing hard labor and loving every minute of it. He seemed a little out of place in a house like this, but at the same time, more at home than anywhere else.

"I was just telling James how lovely this house is," Scotlyn commented, taking a last bite of steak.

"Yup," Sam said, leaning on one elbow and taking a drink of tea. "Was my granny's. I practically grew up here. Never wanted to leave."

"I can see why," she said.

They talked a while longer until he and Scotlyn's father started up about old times and a Laurel Springs that Scotlyn and James had never known because it was before their time.

They talked for a long time, not letting Scotlyn or James get a word in edgewise. James nudged Scotlyn's knee a couple of times with his own, bringing her eyes to his and giving her a conspiratorial smile.

Finally, a little after ten, Scotlyn could feel her eyes beginning to close on their own. She was tired, but didn't want to leave. She wanted to stay beside James, the way she was now.

"You tired?" he asked, putting his hand between her shoulder blades.

She looked over at him and smiled, thinking how nice it would be to just curl up beside him and fall asleep.

"Hey, Dad," he said, nodding toward his father, interrupting their conversation. "This one's tired."

"Oh, I'm sorry, hon!" George said to his daughter, beginning to stand up. "We can go on."

Scotlyn could feel her face turning red with their fussing over her.

"No, no, you two are still catching up," James said. "Why don't I drive Scotlyn home in my car and then if you want, Mr. Carter—"

"George."

"George," James revised. "You could take Scotlyn's car home."

"How will you get to the store tomorrow?" her father asked, turning in Scotlyn's direction.

"Oh," Scotlyn said. James had been planning this out so well. "Well, I could walk," she offered.

"I can come get you and bring you," James said. "If you want."

Scotlyn's father raised an eyebrow slightly but then a look passed over his features that said Scotlyn was a grown woman.

She supposed that it helped that he and James's father got on so well. "Well, I guess that's settled," she said and stood up.

"I'm so glad I got a chance to meet the girl that James hasn't stopped talking about," Sam said as he enveloped her in a hug. "Don't you be a stranger, okay?"

"I won't," she said with a smile, thinking how she liked this man, how great it was that everyone got along, liked each other—how perfect things seemed.

James and George shook hands

"You two be careful," George said.

"We will," James promised. "It was nice meeting you."

"Same here," George said and he and Sam sat back down.

James and Scotlyn could hear them still roaring with laughter as they walked down the back steps and they both laughed to themselves.

"Well, that was a relief," she said, as they slowly walked to James's car. Before they got to it, though, James stopped, looking around at the clear night, the stars overhead, and the crescent moon.

"It's nice out," he observed, and Scotlyn had to agree. It was the warmest night they'd experienced all month. "You want to go for a walk?" he asked.

Scotlyn nodded, and let him lead the way. The night was quiet as they took slow, easy steps along the concrete of the sidewalk.

"Your dad's nice," Scotlyn said.

"He's got you fooled," James said in a joking tone.

They didn't say much to one another after that, but Scotlyn had the feeling that James did want to talk about something. She had a faint feeling of panic that maybe he wanted to break it off between them, but if he were, then why would he bring her there to meet his father, kiss her like he was a soldier returning home from battle? Scotlyn pushed the thought away, tried to enjoy the quiet between them.

Her hand instinctively went to her cross and she ran

it along its cord a few times, the way she always did when she was nervous.

"I hope you don't mind my saying I'd drive you home," he said. She was about to say no, she didn't mind at all, when he continued with, "But I really wanted you to myself."

Scotlyn stopped and dropped her necklace. James stopped, too. He didn't know what she was thinking, was actually nervous for about half a second until she took his hand and laced her fingers with his, looking into his eyes.

"I don't mind," she said.

James stared off into the distance as they resumed their walk. He could take this moment to talk to Scotlyn, to probe information about the robbery out of her. With the intensity of what they were feeling between them, she'd probably talk, for sure. He could take it right to Tommy tonight and then that'd be the end of it.

Yes, he should do that, before this went any further. He knew how to stay strong in situations like this. He'd had to do it on more than one occasion, and talking about the robbery, taking advantage of the delicate moment, was what he needed to do. He was about to start a conversation that would lead to it when he realized that Scotlyn was saying something to him.

"What?" he asked.

"I said I can't believe you never got married," she said.

The words startled him a little, but he didn't mind. In

that part of his life, he had nothing to hide. And he knew exactly what he could say in regards to that that would get Scotlyn to trust him.

He took a breath before beginning. "I don't think I ever really stopped thinking about you since high school. I know we didn't really know each other that well, but I thought about you a lot in the past several years, every time I was with someone else. I knew that was your dad's bookstore when I went in."

Scotlyn didn't know what kind of expression her face held, didn't care.

At the same moment, they moved toward one another until they were again kissing, under the dim light from a streetlamp, not caring if anyone could see them from windows above.

Everything was right, Scotlyn thought, as she pulled back so she could look at him.

"Come home with me," she offered, no nervousness this time. She knew he'd say yes.

Chapter 8

It had seemed almost dreamlike as Scotlyn led him to her room wordlessly, not bothering to turn on lights. They stayed mostly in the darkness, letting only the silvery light of the moon in. When they were in her room, he closed the door almost forcefully behind him, though there was no one else there, and kissed her again, more passionately this time. Then they both gave in to what they had wanted since they'd met years before, not looking back.

When it was over, Scotlyn lay with her back to James, feeling his body curled around hers, his warm breath on her shoulder and neck. She didn't know if he was asleep or awake, but any sleepiness she'd had before was replaced now with an exhaustion laced with rapture, and the feeling that she could stay like that with him forever.

When she awoke the following morning just before dawn, she stretched deeply, feeling some soreness in her shoulders and legs, but loving it nonetheless. She opened her eyes, seeing James propped on his elbow, staring at her. He smiled when she looked at him, a smile she returned, but she couldn't help noticing a hint of sadness in his features.

"Hey," she said.

"Hey," he replied, returning the greeting.

"Something wrong?"

James raised his eyebrows and fixed his expression to a happier one, as if he'd just realized the sadness that had been coming through. "Nope, not at all," he said, running a finger down the side of her face—a gesture that made her giggle, so he did it again.

They stayed like that for a long time until Scotlyn's alarm finally sounded, signaling that it was time to start up another day. She groaned in agony, not wanting the moment to end. Reaching up to turn it off, she turned back to James, who playfully pinned her down.

"How long does it take you to get ready?" he asked into her neck.

"I can manage in half an hour," she said.

James popped his head up to look at the clock, then

back at her with a mischievous grin. "I think that gives us just enough time…"

He leaned in and kissed her.

∽∾∽

James had to do some fast driving to get her to the store so Scotlyn could open it up before her dad got there. She even had to bypass coffee that morning, but James compensated by bringing her a cappuccino after she opened up the store. He set it on the counter and then came around and picked her up, swung her around, and kissed her playfully until she told him he had to stop and get to his dad's garage.

"Okay, okay," he said, hopping up the steps to the store's front door. "I'll talk to you tonight."

Scotlyn smiled at that promise just as the phone rang, taking her back to her day and her work. It was Jane. Scotlyn told her to get down there immediately. Jane, never letting her down when a good romance was in store, burst through the door ten minutes later, hair disheveled, wearing lavender sweatpants paired with a pink T-shirt and slippers.

"Tell me!" she said.

Scotlyn came around the desk to hug her friend and say the words she'd wanted to say to James, but hadn't had the courage to, even after last night and that morning. "I think I'm in love."

Jane screamed so loud that a passerby outside turned to look in the window, sending them into further giggles. Jane stayed for half the morning, even after Scotlyn's dad got there and went to the office, but Scotlyn didn't mention sleeping with James. For some reason, it didn't feel right telling someone else right now, even a close friend. So she just told her friend the details of everything else.

"I seriously don't believe it," Jane said, still about to jump out of her skin with excitement. "It's almost too perfect."

෨෬෬

This is what it feels like to sink into quicksand, James thought as he piloted his Charger toward Tommy's house to give him an update. He wasn't going to mention sleeping with Scotlyn. That hadn't been planned by any means, and, good as it was, it had been a mistake. If this was just a simple relationship, then it'd be different.

James put the car in park and killed the engine, but didn't get out right away. He leaned back against the headrest and closed his eyes, needing just a minute before he had to go in there and put on yet another show. Even though it was a means to an end, he wasn't lying when he told Scotlyn he'd never forgotten her. That shy smile, those damn beautiful eyes, that quiet voice—all of it seemed to find its way into his mind, and mostly when he was just about to take down a score. He never could figure out why that was, but never really thought about the why until he saw her again, until he took her as his lover last night, something he'd promised himself he wouldn't do. And now Scotlyn was probably expecting the two of them to live happily ever after.

James opened his eyes. He sighed once, rubbing his forehead with the heel of his hand, as the pain from his injured, stiff shoulder transferred to his head. He silently cursed as he found nothing but an empty aspirin bottle in his console.

He tugged at his jacket a couple of times before getting out the car and placing the sunglasses over his eyes. May as well get this over with.

Clay opened the door before James even had a chance to knock and James plastered on what he hoped was an easy, charming smile. "Clay."

Don't let them see, he commanded himself and walked through the doorway. It smelled like dirty socks and rotting cheese in the house and James had to breathe in a little at a time through his mouth only.

Clay didn't return the smile, only led James to the living room where Tommy sat in front of a basketball game drinking a beer.

"Jimmy," Tommy said in cheerful tone that made James want to hurl him out the window. "How's it going?"

"Great," James said, sitting across from Tommy and

trying to look comfortable, not bothering to remove his sunglasses.

"You have a certain look about you this morning," Tommy pried.

James forced himself to smile. "Well, I've been keeping up pretty steadily with Scotlyn," he said. "She trusts me, I can tell you that. It'll only be a matter of time before she breaks."

"Keeping up pretty good," Tommy said, taking a swig from his beer. "I'll say."

James felt a stab in his solar plexus. "What do you mean?" he asked, keeping his voice steady.

"You spent *all* of last night at that girl's house," Tommy began, cutting his eyes over to James and half-grinning suggestively. "Moving in pretty quick, aren't you?"

James looked through Tommy. "I thought I told you—"

"Hey, Jeff just happened to be passing by her house, saw your car there last night, saw it again this morning. We weren't spying, honest."

James noticed for the first time that Jeff wasn't around. "Well," he said, standing up and rubbing his palms together. "I guess you're pretty satisfied, then, that things are progressing?"

Tommy's eyes were still on the television as he nodded, and turned his head to the side. "Yup."

"Good," James said and turned to make his way

toward the front door before things got out of hand. "I'd better go to my dad's garage and help him out before my cover gets blown."

"Hey," Tommy yelled, bringing him back. He smiled as he asked, "Was she any good?"

James paused for a second, considering whether or not to take his gun from the holster underneath his jacket and shoot Tommy. Instead, he turned and walked out the front door, hearing Tommy chuckle behind him.

When he got outside, he made a quick phone call to someone he begrudged almost as much as he did Tommy. He knew what he had to do. He had to end this, now, before it got even more out of hand, before Scotlyn's life was in real danger.

∽↗∽↗

It felt like someone was banging his skull with a sledgehammer from the inside, Jeff thought as he sat on the park bench, his sunglasses shielding his bloodshot eyes from the sun. It probably had not been such a good idea to stay at that strip club until three in the morning and then spend the rest of it with that nice little bottle of vodka he kept stashed in his trunk. He'd already had three Jack Daniels at the bar and had shelled out probably several hundred dollars in the VIP room at the club.

And not one of those broads had taken him up on his offer of coming back to his place for a more-than-generous tip. They had just shucked their clothes and teased him all night long.

Jeff shook his head and caught a glimpse of his reflection in a store's window across the way. He sat hunched over, his skin pale and sweaty, even in the coolness of the late morning.

Huh, he thought. No wonder they hadn't come back with him.

But that was all going to change soon. When they closed up this deal with this Jimmy character, he'd be on his way to bigger and better things, would get a nice car, clothes, a mansion somewhere and no woman would ever say no to him again.

Jeff sat back on the bench, contemplating as he watched the bookstore across the way, looking for signs of *her*. Yeah, when this was all over, he'd take care of Tommy and Clay just fine, though he hadn't decided how just yet. He didn't need them. *He* was a leader, not Tommy! They were just a means to an end. Jeff would get his own crew, and make some serious money. Yes. That's what he'd do. He was smart, and he had ideas! They just didn't listen to him.

The little dark-haired girl came out of the store then, calling one last thing to someone inside as she did. Jeff watched as she crossed the street, waved to a car that let her pass by, and went into a little sandwich shop, probably to pick up some lunch. There was a bounce in her step today, Jeff noticed, an energy that had not been there before, and he hardly had to wonder just what was making her so happy.

Screw Jimmy, he thought, looking at the sandwich shop's entrance, though he couldn't see anything. He knew the bastard had told them not to stalk her, but Jeff would be damned if he did anything that guy told him. He was moving too slow!

She was bound to remember Jeff's face any day now and she was probably going to go running straight to the cops! Hell, she might even be playing Jimmy. Might have a game of her own going.

Jeff pulled a package of cigarettes out of his jacket pocket and lit one, watching as she came out of the sandwich shop, carrying two to-go boxes. She was hot, no doubt about it, Jeff thought, as he exhaled smoke. He still thought about just moving in on her himself, just taking her in the middle of the night, having his way with her, and then doing away with her.

Jeff flicked an ash and then took another drag, watching the store with his head down. Maybe that's exactly what he would do.

Chapter 9

Despite the rain and the darkness that was all but blocking his vision, James piloted his Charger faster along the highway. He was already a long way from Laurel Springs, and he had an even longer plane ride ahead of him.

It was harder this time, he thought, as he steered around a mini-van and pressed down on the accelerator. His cell vibrated on the console beside him and, with the light that illuminated his caller ID, he saw the very reason why it was so much harder this time around. Scotlyn, calling him from over thirty miles away. Of course, she was calling him. He hadn't called her in two days, having spent the time trying to figure a way out of this that would end this deal right now and leave Scotlyn safe at the same time. But nothing came to him. All of his years of experience and still nothing, damn it. These guys were expecting a huge payout, and even if James emptied his savings and presented it to them right now, there was no way he could ensure that they wouldn't harm Scotlyn, anyway, just for the fun of it. Not to mention that Martin, the only man who could help him, would be furious.

James shook his head. Scotlyn would not be hurt, even if he had to leave her right now.

Finally giving up and calling Martin again last night, James told him of his problem, and Martin, knowing this was something they needed to discuss face to face, told him to get to DC right now.

James tightened his grip on the steering wheel as he took the exit for the airport, trying to ignore the beep on his phone that let him know he had a new voicemail.

 ȔƆȔ

James didn't call Scotlyn or come over that night. Or the next night. Or the next. She was successful in forcing herself not to call him again, but not in worrying over why he didn't at least call. Lying in bed that night around midnight, staring at the ceiling and knowing she was nowhere near sleep, she scolded herself for acting like a scorned teenager.

She suddenly thought about a guy in school named Ward. He had brown hair that was forever disheveled, pockmarked skin, and had a penchant for sarcastic remarks and playing the guitar. They'd never spoken, but she remembered how he'd chased relentlessly after a girl who arrived from some other town midway into the school year. What was her name? Catherine? Caitlyn? For some reason, Scotlyn was angry with herself for not remembering. Ward was like a bloodhound chasing a fox when he went after Catherine/Caitlyn, a girl as quiet as Scotlyn, obviously shy as she usually kept her head in her book, with her wiry blonde hair falling over her face. She apparently wasn't used to the attention he was showering upon her and giggled at his lame sarcasm, mistaking it for honest jokes.

Then one day, Ward stopped chasing her, started directing the remarks at Catherine/Caitlyn when she tried to talk to him. It didn't take a genius to figure out what had happened between them. And while Ward went on to become a pseudo-Don Juan, Catherine/Caitlyn became even more of a social pariah than before. No one talked to her, only about her. Scotlyn caught wind sometimes, hearing words like "gross" and "slut" when Catherine/Caitlyn's name was mentioned.

"Just a lonely girl," Scotlyn said out loud. A girl who'd just made a mistake and given in to her loneliness, and to a moron desperate to lose his virginity.

But James is not *Ward, not by a long shot*, she

reminded herself and said a quick prayer filled with gratefulness for that fact. James wasn't like Ward or any of the other guys, even today, who'd chase after girls simply to get laid and then discard them.

She turned over in her bed and shut her eyes, trying to force herself to sleep, but it didn't happen.

Well, she mused. *At least it's not fear keeping me awake this time.*

And at least it was busy at work the next morning. Every time Scotlyn got a moment to step behind the counter, someone would ask for help in finding a book or would purchase one, halting any thoughts or worries that were on their way to her mind. By the time noon rolled around, the store was all but abandoned. Her dad was taking the day off again, and it was just her and her thoughts. Bad combination.

Scotlyn couldn't help it. She pulled her phone out of her purse and checked to see if she had any missed calls.

There were none.

Sighing, she sat on the chair behind the front desk, looking at calls from several days ago, seeing James's number. Her thumb hovered over his number and just a second before she pushed it, someone opened the front door of the shop, taking her back to reality.

ⓔⓢⓔⓢ

Not thinking about someone could be as hard as

thinking about them, Scotlyn observed as she finished counting down the register, locked the money in the safe, and locked the back office. She ran her hand along the long mahogany countertop as she slowly walked past it and switched off the lights when she got to the front door, leaving the little lamp on the counter burning.

She closed the front door behind her, locked it, and double-checked it before turning and looking around a moment. She took in the pale sky of the dusk hour, the lights that were already twinkling on the trees in the square.

Her car was right there in front of her, but instead of unlocking it and getting in to drive home, she twirled her keys around her slim fingers for a second before dropping them in her purse and putting her hands in her pockets. She turned to walk the one mile back home, looking down at the sidewalk, at her feet as she took slow steps, one right after the other.

Her job had kept her from dwelling on James and the fact that he'd never called like he'd promised he would, and now it was like all the thinking she hadn't done was crashing into her.

Every thought or reason of why he hadn't called tumbled over one another in her mind, making her rub her forehead with the heel of her hand.

Had he been in an accident? Had she *displeased* him some way? Did he just get what he wanted from her and leave for good?

She shook her head as sense told her, *we settled that last night, remember?*

Scotlyn looked around, thinking, she could just casually drive her car by his father's garage and see if he was there, right? That wouldn't be too obvious, right?

Stalker, she scolded herself. She was a long way away from the bookstore now and was tired. She may have had enough energy to do something like that if she were about ten or so years younger, but not now.

It's only been a few days, she thought as she turned down her street, the sky getting darker now. You're an adult, not a kid. There could be a thousand little reasons why he hadn't called, none of which are probably life or relationship-threatening.

She really didn't think something bad had happened. Wouldn't his father have contacted her in some way if there had?

Ah, screw it, she thought as she took her phone out of her purse, not missing a step as she neared her house. She found James's number in her phone and this time, without hesitation, pressed it, ready for whatever.

It rang three times before she heard his voice on the other end say, "Hello?"

She was about to say something back when she realized the voice wasn't just coming from within the phone. It was louder, closer.

Scotlyn looked up and all around and then—there he was.

She stopped where she was, looking at him sitting there on her front stoop with his one arm resting on his knees and the other holding his phone to his ear.

Hallucination? Scotlyn wondered for a moment, but then James partially lifted a couple of fingers in a small wave. His expression didn't change, and he didn't move otherwise, as if he'd encountered a wild animal and was just taking his time, not making any sudden moves that might make the animal attack him.

Finally, they both hung up and replaced their phones at nearly the same moment. It took Scotlyn a long time to make the short walk up to her stoop. When she got to James, she let her purse drop from her shoulder before catching it with her hand and having a seat beside him. He was cold, she could see, and she wondered just how long he'd been sitting there. They sat in silence for a long time as an occasional car passed them by.

"It's been a while," Scotlyn finally said in a voice that was quiet even to her.

James's profile was severe, but he half smiled at her words.

"Everything okay?" Scotlyn didn't know what else to say.

"Yeah," he answered. "You?"

She shrugged as she put her hands between her knees, realizing how cold they were. "Been a little worried."

He looked at her, then, almost sadly, and the alarm

bells started going off. She'd seen that look before. "I'm sorry for not calling," he finally said.

Scotlyn didn't bat an eye.

"There *is* something I should tell you," he began.

This is it, she thought, readying herself for a speech she'd heard thousands of times, but then thought about how, no matter how many times a person heard the same pathetic words or excuses, they could never fully prepare themselves for the train that was about to hit them. She waited, but he didn't speak again, or couldn't, maybe.

After a moment, he reached up and ran a finger down the side of her face, and she felt the electricity again. Did he feel it too? She didn't know, and the thought that she didn't really know him at all returned.

But, as Scotlyn continued to look at his eyes, that were still mysterious and somehow sad again today, she realized how much she wanted to know him.

"But…" he said, clearly unable to find the words to tell her what he felt he should.

"But," Scotlyn repeated, though not as a question.

He looked at her again. "I'm so glad I ran into you in your bookstore that day," he said.

She could feel her nerves easing just a little, could feel something shift inside her mind. Something was on his mind, obviously, but it didn't seem like it was something that would affect them, and if it was something he was having trouble telling her, something that could wait, then it was all right.

Still, she had to test it.

She stood up and turned a little toward the front door. James stayed where he was, aware that he had not yet been invited in. She stretched her hand out a little, offering it to him and, after a moment, he took it and followed her inside.

She didn't bother turning on the lights as she closed and locked the door behind her, just dropped her purse on the floor and put her arms around her lover, a gesture he returned almost before she initiated it, holding her like she'd fade away any second.

"Maybe you can tell me some other time," she said into his neck before leading him to her room.

Later that night, exhausted and drifting toward sleep, Scotlyn wasn't sure, but she thought she heard James say that he loved her.

സൗ

It was raining hard when Scotlyn opened her eyes again, and she smiled. Waking up to rainfall, knowing she had nowhere to go and nothing to do at the moment was one of the simple joys she got out of life. She stretched until she felt it deep in her muscles and turned over, but didn't find James.

Oh great, she thought to herself. *He did it again.* The space beside her on the bed wasn't even warm, meaning it had been a while since he'd been beside her. Scotlyn shook her head as she sat up and drew her knees to her chest. Funny thing was, she wasn't all that mad or hurt, though she wasn't sure why. She was just pushing the covers off her when she realized she smelled coffee and saw his jacket still draped over the chair beside her dresser. Half-smiling, she pulled on some pajama pants and a thin flannel robe, feeling the chill that she'd become accustomed to feeling in her poorly-insulated house.

Sure enough, James was in the kitchen. He'd dressed in jeans and was standing over her breakfast table looking at something in the newspaper as he took long, slow sips from his coffee cup.

"Hey," she finally said.

He turned and nodded at her. "Hope I didn't wake you."

"No, the rain did that just fine," she said, opening the glass cabinet that housed her mugs. She fixed herself a cup of coffee and had a seat at the table. She looked outside for a long time before James took a seat across from her.

"You find some aspirin?" she asked, taking a sip, remembering his shoulder.

He smiled, still looking at the table. "Sweet girl," he said instead of answering her question. He brought his coffee cup to his mouth and looked at the steady rainfall.

"I thought you were gone," she said, bringing a hand up to rest on her neck.

"Hope it's okay that I'm not."

She smiled. "You make good coffee. I don't think anyone's ever made me coffee before."

He raised an eyebrow as he now looked at her.

"Not that I've had a lot of overnight guests," she said quickly, feeling the burning of embarrassment in her cheeks.

He laughed for the first time since coming back to her. "Just teasing you," he said.

He took another sip of his own coffee and then thanked her for the compliment. Scotlyn watched him as he looked out the window at the rain that was heavier now, and she considered all the unsaid things between them. She wondered if he'd tell her anything about what he'd only mentioned, in the briefest of words, last night. Scotlyn took a sip of the good coffee. She'd never been one to push someone, thinking that if someone really wanted to tell her something, they would. And she wasn't going to push James, thinking about how he didn't push her to tell him about the most traumatic thing that had happened to her in recent months.

Scotlyn looked at the mail strewn on the table before her, as some certainty settled in. She loved James. She'd known that for a while now, had been intimate with him in a physical way, but not in an entirely honest way, and suddenly something seemed inappropriate, something she needed to fix.

"There's something I should probably tell you, too,"

she said. She set her coffee cup down and folded her arms on the table before her. He looked her way, and she could see the worry on his face, so she smiled. "Don't worry, there's no one else in my life."

He didn't smile back at her, and didn't encourage her to continue.

"A few months before we met up again," she said, looking at the table now. "Something happened to me."

She rushed through telling him everything: the robbery, the kidnapping, the escape, the robber's threat, the constant fear, seeing a psychiatrist. He never said a word, never interrupted her, and was so still she half-wondered if he'd heard a word she'd said, or if she'd said anything out loud at all. Finally, eternal minutes after she finished her story, he got up from his chair, moved in front of her, and held out both of his hands, which she took. Instead of pulling her to her feet, he knelt in front of her, and put his face over her hands, almost like he was asking forgiveness. When he looked up at her again, his eyes were fierce, and Scotlyn was almost afraid.

He put one hand on the side of her neck. "Nothing like that is *ever* going to happen to you again."

Scotlyn smiled but couldn't look him in the eye. "You were always good at so many things, but you can't predict the future. Those guys are still out there. How do you know they won't come back?"

"Because I—"

James began his sentence quickly, like he was going

to give her a good and knowing reason why those guys wouldn't be back to hurt her, but as quickly as he began he stopped himself short.

He got up and turned away from her.

Okay, she thought, but didn't know what to say.

He rubbed his face a little before turning back to her, holding his hand up. "Because I—I'll take care of you. I promise."

The kitchen darkened as the rain started to come down more heavily all around them outside.

Chapter 10

It was mid-April, and they had barely left one another's side. Scotlyn smiled as she looked at the ceiling, enjoying a lazy Saturday morning in James's bed. Ever since he'd come back to her that night, they'd been seeing each other four and five times a week, going to movies, for walks late at night, for runs in the morning, to Roman's for dinner.

Their times together frequently lasted well into the night and they'd ended up staying over at one another's houses on many occasions, eventually leaving things like toothbrushes, shampoo, and various articles of clothing. Scotlyn remembered waking up one morning and finding a T-shirt James had lost tucked into her sheets and smiling at the scent he'd left behind on it.

He hadn't left her again, and still hadn't revealed the reason he had before. They hadn't talked about it or the robbery again. For some reason, all of that seemed to be getting farther away in Scotlyn's mind, a feeling she really loved.

It was like they were focusing on just being together, happy. No expectations or conflicts. It was as if the past didn't matter so much anymore. She hadn't even had to see Dr. Brenner as much, who told her she was looking better with each session.

"I guess love agrees with me," she'd admitted to him.

"Agrees with me," she now said out loud.

"What?" James asked.

"Nothing," she said, shaking her head.

"Where are you?" he asked.

He was lying on his back, too, right beside her, though she could've sworn he was farther away from the moment than she.

"Right here with you," she said. "You?"

"I'm here," he said.

"Could've fooled me," she said, turning over to face him and tucking her arm underneath her head. He didn't turn to face her, just stayed there with his hands laced behind his head, looking at the ceiling.

"Hey," he said all of a sudden.

"Hey," she said.

He bounced around in bed to face her, an excited expression on his face now. "Come away with me," he said.

"Away?" Scotlyn repeated, raising her eyebrows. "Where?"

"Anywhere," he said. "The beach, the mountains, California, or Montana—"

"Whoa!" Scotlyn said, sitting up.

"I've got money," he said, sitting up with her and rubbing her back. "I'll pay for everything."

"It's not that," she said. "It's just…I don't know…"

"You took off before when you were only twenty-two," he reminded her.

"Yeah, but that took months of planning."

"Well, you were alone," he said. "Now you have me."

Scotlyn looked at him, smiled, and leaned over to kiss him.

"Yeah," she said. "But…"

James waited, his hand still on her back.

"My dad," she said. "The store…I don't know if I can leave him."

James sighed and rubbed her back some more. How she wanted to say yes, but didn't know who she could get to help her.

"How is it *you* can take off like that?" she asked.

James shrugged. "Dad's pretty well got everything

under control at the garage, hired another guy to come in a few times a week. He could spare me."

"Hmm," Scotlyn said. She thought about asking Jane if she could help out. Her father knew Jane and trusted her with everything if he couldn't come in. Jane could probably use the extra money, too. It would take some training, but maybe they could work it out.

"I don't know," she said. "Let me do some thinking. Can I let you know tonight?"

James leaned in and kissed her before settling back into the pillows and pulling her with him. "Sure."

They stayed together like that until Scotlyn could feel her stomach starting to growl and she realized how long it had been since she'd eaten anything. Last night, they'd bypassed dinner altogether, opting instead to just come back to James's house and to his bed.

"Hey," she said.

"Hey."

"Would you do something for me?" she asked.

"Yup."

"Would you cook breakfast for me? I'm starving."

"I'm a terrible cook. Why don't we just go out?"

"Because I'm way too comfortable," she said, sitting up and winking at him. "I trust you."

James laughed. "Well, I guess I can try."

"Good," she said, nestling back into the pillows. He leaned forward to kiss her once before getting out of bed and throwing on a T-shirt and jeans.

"I'm pretty sure you don't need to get dressed to cook breakfast—"

"I don't have anything I can cook," he said, pulling on some shoes. He grabbed his keys off the dresser. "I'll be back soon."

"I'll be here," she said.

She heard him close the back door behind him and stared at the ceiling for a while, enjoying the moment until deciding to go ahead and make some coffee. She sat up and stretched a long moment before pulling on her jeans and top and walking lazily to the kitchen. She found a bag of coffee grounds in the refrigerator, filled the pot with water, and set it.

She was standing with her arms crossed when she heard the back door open again, a little more slowly this time. Knowing that James couldn't have been to the store and back by now, she called, "You forget something?" without looking back.

A large arm grabbed her then and, before she could react, a cloth covered her mouth. She remembered breathing in to scream, but then she became instantly drowsier than she'd ever been. Her head fell onto a foreign shoulder and, before she could get scared, everything turned to black.

☙☙☙

James pushed open the back door of his house and

kicked it closed behind him. He saw the coffee pot on but there was no sign of Scotlyn. He set the bags on the counter and went to the bedroom, but she wasn't there. Neither were the clothes she'd shed on the floor last night. He paused, touching the doorframe a minute before turning to the bathroom, though something was already turning over in his mind.

As he'd suspected, the bathroom was empty. Scotlyn wasn't there, he knew, but he called her name anyway, hoping, just hoping, that maybe he was wrong. He turned in a full circle, feeling the world spin.

No.

He got his cell out of his pocket and dialed her number, but he could hear her phone ringing from his nightstand as his own rang in his ear and so he snapped it closed.

"Scotlyn!" he screamed now.

That's when his eyes landed on the envelope that had been strategically placed beside the coffee pot. It was an unopened piece of junk mail, some come-on for cable services. He saw all too familiar handwriting as he looked at it from across the room, though he didn't yet know what it said. He took the room in two steps and grabbed the envelope, holding in front of his face. There was only one line:

If you want her back, you know who to call.

James stared at the handwriting for a long time. His expression never changed, but he could feel something inside him shift. A rage, one he'd learned to control and channel into his work, was building now, threatening to tear him apart from the inside out. He crumpled the envelope, his hand hard and, shaking now, and threw it across the room. Then all of the bags he'd set on the counter, the coffee pot, and couple of other things crashed to the floor. He turned, and slammed his fist into the wall in the hallway without missing a step to the bathroom.

Calm down, he told himself and ran the tap in the sink. He was going to have to clear his mind if he was going to get Scotlyn back. He splashed the icy water over his face and hair several times before returning to his bedroom, not bothering to dry his face. He went to his walk-in closet and pushed the wall in where the secret hideaway was that only he knew about.

He pulled out his shotgun and the box of bullets he kept in there, kicked the door closed again, and went back to the living room. He thought he had the rage under control now, but before he knew it, he slammed the end of the shotgun into a lamp and sent it crashing into a wall before it fell to floor in a million little pieces. He kicked the coffee table across the room, letting the rage consume him now, knowing he'd have to keep his wits about him when he confronted these guys.

Simply killing them wasn't an option and going in there feeling the way he did now, he was liable to do just that. Or if he went in there unfocused and angry, Tommy,

Clay, and Jeff could very well overpower him and he really wouldn't be able to save Scotlyn.

James set the gun down, walked over to the wall, and pushed both palms into it, trying to let the thoughts of her calm him down. But all he could do was wonder what they were doing to her, and if she was safe.

Chapter 11

Idiot!" Tommy said, circling Jeff, who stood with his arms crossed, watching through the mirrored window the woman he'd kidnapped earlier that morning and tied to a chair in the empty room. She sat motionless, scared most likely, as she leaned forward slightly, her head down, a blindfold over her eyes.

Tommy could see a faint smirk on Jeff's face and knocked him good upside the head. Jeff flinched and turned to face his boss, as if he was about to hit him back. Clay stepped up beside Tommy, and Jeff thought twice, though the fury remained in his eyes.

"Do you have *any* idea what this is going to cost us?"

Tommy went on, ignoring Jeff's rage. "How mad Jimmy is, probably, at this very minute? I'm surprised he hasn't come in here, guns blazing, and blown us all to pieces by now."

"He was taking too long, having a little too much fun while we just sat here, broke, waiting, and worrying," Jeff retorted. "She was going to go to the authorities sooner or later. He wasn't getting it done—"

Tommy silenced him by knocking him across the face. That was too much for little Jeff. This time, he drew his fist back to punch Tommy in the face, but Clay grabbed him by the elbow.

"Enough," Clay said to Jeff, then looked back at Tommy. "We have to fix this."

"That's right," Tommy said, without ever taking his eyes off Jeff. "That job in North Carolina is probably gone to hell right now, and so's our chance to get out of this town!"

"No," Jeff said, yanking his arm from Clay's grip and pointing at the window. "This shows what we're capable of, that he can't mess with us."

"Idiot!" Tommy shouted again, turning and punching the wall, wanting just to beat Jeff to a pulp.

"We have her now," Jeff continued. "And from what I saw, Jimmy was obviously doing more than just playing her. The guy's fallen for her big time, and that means he'll do anything to get her back, give us *anything* we want."

Tommy shook his head. Jimmy could be stupid when it came to women, yeah, and Tommy knew that, for the most part, Jeff was right. Jimmy had definitely fallen for this girl.

But he wasn't stupid when it came to deals. He'd negotiate, but if they threatened her even more, Jimmy would probably bring in some of the other groups he'd worked with in the past, guys who wouldn't have a problem killing the three of them while Jimmy got his girl out of there.

Hell, he might do that anyway. And as for that job in North Carolina and Tommy getting a better life…well, he just hoped he could smooth things over.

"You aren't as smart as you think," Tommy said, turning and walking from the room. It was time to call Jimmy and see if he could fix this.

෧෩෧

James sat on the couch, looking out the window across from him, the mess from everything he'd broken still surrounding him. His shotgun was in his lap, his cellular at his side. He'd already been in touch with Martin, who was on his way this very minute. James knew the next step was to wait, to let them contact him so they could negotiate terms, so they'd relax and think they had the upper hand. But if they pushed it, if they harmed Scotlyn—

James's cell started to vibrate on the couch next to him and he turned to look at it. The number flashing was Tommy's. James breathed in.

Calm, he warned himself, hit the recorder that was plugged into his phone, and opened it with a tight hand.

"Tommy," he said into the receiver.

"Hey, Jimmy," Tommy said. "How're you doing?"

James wanted to crush the phone in his hand and hurl it across the room. Instead, he closed his eyes and said, very slowly, "You have something that belongs to me."

"Yeah," Tommy said. "Sorry about that. Jeff—he got a little anxious."

James tried to breathe in and out, but his chest felt like it was going to cave in, the way it did when he ran too hard and too fast for too long.

"Well," James said. "When can I expect to get her back?"

James knew the protocol, knew what was coming next, and waited.

"Love to do that for you right away," Tommy said, drawing this out like he was in control. "We need something from you first, though, if you don't mind."

"Tell me."

"Well, you know a lot of people from a lot of places…" Tommy let the sentence hang for a minute. "Figure you might know someone who could get a hold of some truth serum. You bring it here, give her a nice little dose, question her in front of us."

Oh, geez, how stupid can you get, James thought, but instead answered, "All right."

He knew that Martin could get the serum for him, but that it would probably take a day. He told Tommy this.

"Well," Tommy began his answer. "Guess we'll have to baby-sit her, then."

"Let me talk to her," James commanded.

"Not so fast," Tommy said. "There's one other thing. We want what you promised us."

"You think I'm still going to work with you after this?" James asked, knowing he was pushing it now, that he needed to watch himself.

"We're getting rid of Jeff, soon, *permanently*," Tommy said in a much lower voice.

James guessed that Jeff was somewhere within close range of earshot. "And I should believe you?"

Tommy laughed on his end. "Do you have much of a choice?"

James was silent. Tommy took that as his cue to move on. "After we're satisfied that the little bitch knows nothing—"

"Don't call her that again," James interrupted.

"All right, Jimmy," Tommy said, conceding to that demand. "After we're satisfied that this *girl* knows nothing, we'll meet at another location, collect on the deal we made on the metals factory. No one gets hurt. Clay and I will take care of Jeff as a way to compensate for what he did."

James waited.

"And then we give you proof of that and talk about the mark in North Carolina," Tommy finished.

James was silent for a moment. "Fine."

"All right then," Tommy said, sounding satisfied. "Good doing business with you."

"Wait a minute," James said.

Tommy didn't speak, but didn't hang up.

"I want to talk to her."

"Oh, right," Tommy said, remembering. "I'll let you hear her, but you don't say a word."

James didn't say whether or not he agreed to do that, but he could hear Tommy moving around and footsteps. There was a loud buzzing sound and then the squeak of a door opening.

"Hello?" Scotlyn's voice, haggard and shaky, called out. "Is someone there?"

The door clanged shut and Tommy returned to the phone.

"Satisfied?" he asked.

"I'll be there tomorrow," James said. "Two o'clock."

He hung up the phone and ran his hands roughly through his hair, holding them there and resting his elbows on his knees. *Hold on, Scotlyn.*

જીલજી

Martin Blake, nearing sixty, was a short, stocky man

with hair receding clear to the middle of his head. He had more than a few extra pounds around his mid-section, enough to keep him from buttoning the jacket on his gray suit, but he walked with a fast gait, and swung his arms almost ferociously as he strode up the back steps to James's house and entered without knocking. He found James where he knew he'd be—sitting on the couch, waiting, staring that intense stare he did when he was in that zone of his.

"Hey, kid," Martin said, patting James once on the shoulder as he came around and took a seat on the chair opposite the couch. James didn't respond, but Martin wasn't offended. They could hardly be classified as friends.

Martin had caught James working a score alone in Los Angeles years earlier when Martin had been a little younger and in a lot better shape. He'd told the kid that he could come to work undercover for the FBI to help bring down other crews or go to jail.

James, being no fool, had grudgingly agreed to work for them and, since then, he and Martin had been in almost constant contact.

Martin surveyed the mess as he waited for James to begin and knew that this was not good, that James was in over his head.

James finally filled him in on everything, handing over the recordings of his phone conversations, all the while never looking at Martin.

"All right," Martin said, taking the recorder. "I'll make sure a crew is out here first thing tomorrow morning. No can do on the truth serum, though."

James shot him a glare. "Why's that?"

"It's against FBI policies. Sorry, kid. We don't work that way."

"Tommy asked for it. He's liable to kill Scotlyn if I don't deliver. What am I going to do?"

Martin sat back in the chair and sighed. "What would you do if you gave her truth serum and she says she does remember Jeff's face? How will you get yourself and her out of that?"

James didn't answer.

"I'll get you a saline injection."

"Saline?"

"That's right. Administer that. She'll be fine. No effects."

"You're sure about that?"

"Positive."

"What about Tommy?"

Martin threw his hands up. "What about Tommy? He asked for the truth serum, which tells me he doesn't know how to get it and most likely doesn't even know what it would look like. Trust me. Give her the saline. Tommy will be none the wiser."

James sighed and looked at the floor. He could only hope like hell that Martin was right. He couldn't think about what he would do if anything happened to Scotlyn.

Martin studied James from across the room. "You did the right thing, kid."

"You keep telling me that," James answered, still looking straight ahead.

"It's true."

"What's the ultimate plan?" James asked. "When I make the drop off to these guys?"

"I'll have to talk with whoever else they send over, but bottom line, we're going to take them *alive* if we can. Our men will be there, place them under arrest, and make it look like you just got away."

"I want your assurance that she won't be hurt," James said with finality.

"We'll do everything we can, obviously—"

"No," James said. "I want a guarantee. I've been the FBI's pawn for years, now, and have never asked for a thing or gotten a thing in return. I want Scotlyn out of there safe and sound."

Martin raised an eyebrow. "What you've gotten here, *Jimmy*, is freedom—freedom you are damn well lucky to have."

James looked at him for the first time.

"And that you will continue to have if you play by our rules. Do you understand?"

James didn't answer, but Martin didn't expect him to. Martin sighed. "Fine. I'll take that as a 'yes.'"

∞

Scotlyn breathed hard, though forcefully slow, trying to focus, trying to gather scraps of information about where she was by smelling and feeling the air around her. She already had a pretty good idea of who was doing this—the men who'd robbed the bank a few months ago because, really, what were the odds? What she didn't know, though was nonetheless grateful for, was why they didn't just kill her.

Still, she couldn't be absolutely certain and just tried to focus on doing what they told her as quickly and quietly as possible. It was strange. She'd always pictured herself scared in a situation like this, desperately trying to keep her heart and breathing under control, but it wasn't that hard to do either. It just took a little concentration, and the *knowledge*, not the *thought*, that she was going to get out of here.

Maybe I'm becoming a seasoned captive, she told herself, trying to laugh internally at her own weak joke because if she didn't, if she let the situation in, it might take her over and give her an attack from which she might not recover. She couldn't think about James, or her father, or Jane, because if she did, sudden images would come to mind of them worried or anxious or worse, their faces contorted with outrage and horror as police told them of her death. No. She had to keep her mind on a narrow path.

Her memory was still blurry of how this all happened. She just remembered blacking out, struggling against the strong angry hands and arms that were holding her, and then waking in this hard wooden and steel chair, her wrists tied down to the arms of it and her ankles tied to the legs.

She had a blindfold over her eyes, tied tight enough for her not to know if there was a window in the room, if it was day or night, or even how much time had passed. She'd slipped into unconsciousness a couple of times, though it was impossible to tell how much sleep she'd gotten. The room was cool and damp, too, with a metallic and musty smell to it that creeped her out and made her wonder if there were rats or other creatures lurking around. Mercifully, though, if there were, she never felt them around her feet.

There was a buzz from several feet away and Scotlyn heard a metal clang as a door opened. She lifted her head toward it, the way she had done much earlier—or maybe it wasn't so much earlier—and had called out, "Hello? Is anyone there?" There was no answer except the door clanging shut once more.

Scotlyn didn't speak this time, only waited as heavy footsteps approached her. Large hands began to work at the ropes around her arms and legs.

"Get up," a burly yet quiet voice said to her and Scotlyn eased her way to her feet, noting the tingling in the back of her legs and the stiff aches running up and down her back as if they were saying, *It's about time you moved around.*

Someone pulled off the blindfold with a yank that took out some of her hair.

"Ouch," she said instinctively, putting her hands on the back of her head, the fiery sting still pulsating along her scalp.

Everything was blurry for a moment, but she focused on the floor, seeing it was concrete, as were the walls. The room was dim, lit only by a single bulb hanging over the chair. There were no windows, except one of those police ones on one wall, designed to let someone see in from one side, but not the other.

They've been watching me, Scotlyn thought suddenly.

"Let's go," said the voice.

Out of the corner of her eye, she caught a glimpse of a man with a ski mask covering his face. She quickly turned her head away, not wanting to look at the voice's owner, thinking it best to just keep her head down. Something hard jabbed into her back, and she stumbled forward.

A gun, she thought, but still tried to focus on the floor before her. They reached the door, a loud buzzer sounded, and a hand reached around her to open it. He let her walk through first, though there was no gentlemanly kindness to the gesture. They walked down a hall that was as dimly lit as the room she'd been in. It had been painted a cream color a long time ago, though it was now peeling from all angles. It was stuffier in there, warmer.

"Stop," the man said when they got about halfway down the hall and opened another door.

"You have five minutes," he told her as he pushed her through that door and Scotlyn looked up for the first time, at her own reflection. She was in a tiny, dingy bathroom. A little toilet with a black seat was against the wall and the sink before her was partially covered in dirt. The mirror, she noticed, was cracked right along the reflection of her face. Scotlyn could make out the indentations from where the blindfold had been and touched them before remembering her captor's warning. She quickly used the facilities and rinsed her hands, though there was no soap. She splashed some of the water in her face and drank a few handfuls, knowing she had to stay hydrated if nothing else.

Then, suddenly, and without control, there it was. The panic that had been threatening to rise in her chest, that had been lurking around way back there inside her mind, just waiting for the right moment. Scotlyn could feel her heart pick up, and she grasped either side of the sink.

Stop it, she commanded the panic. *Get away from me.*

She looked at herself. She was not going to break.

She heard a bang at the door.

"Time's up," a voice shouted.

Scotlyn turned off the water and took a last look at her cracked reflection.

James, she thought uncontrollably. Her next thought came to her without reason or knowledge of why—*Help me*.

ᏋᏒᏋᏒ

"All right," Martin said, pacing the other side of the dining room, his hands laced across the back of his neck. "We clear?"

James nodded while Rick and Lewis, two other agents Martin had called in said "Yes" in unison.

James didn't want anyone else there, but he knew that Rick and Lewis were needed, especially one of them, anyway, when they made the drop off. They'd arrived that very morning in a large black SUV. Rick was still fit but a little older with gray in his beard and hair, and Lewis, younger, about James's age, and more built. They were both seasoned, obviously, knew their jobs, and did them with little questioning, which put James at ease. They weren't amateurs, and that was good.

James turned the plastic-enclosed syringe containing the saline over and over in his hand. Martin was going on about something else now, though James barely heard him. It was closing in on 1:30, his appointed time to leave to go meet these guys and make sure that Scotlyn was all right, though he knew he couldn't stay with her for long. He couldn't show signs of weakness, not in front of Tommy or Clay, and especially not in front of Jeff.

"James?" Martin called him back.

James looked at the man who'd captured him all those years ago.

"Time to go," Martin said, and James nodded, putting the syringe in the inner pocket of his leather jacket.

He strapped on his ankle holster, knowing they might search him for a weapon, but only from the waist up. These guys were pretty good at what they did, but they were still dumb enough to miss a few things.

"Get in there," Martin said, repeating the day's mission. "Give her the injection, find some way to communicate to her what she needs to say to give them the information they want. Tell them you'll contact them tomorrow when you have the money, which is—"

"In transit now," James said. "My fence, who I had entrusted it with, is bringing it."

"And is…"

"Two hundred twenty-five thousand."

"Good," Martin said then, almost as encouragement, added, "You'll do fine."

James put his sunglasses on and turned away.

"Hey," Martin said, making James turn around. "She is worth this, isn't she?"

Martin hadn't been very pleased when James told him about the way he'd modified the deal with these three idiots on a dime, just to ensure that a girl he'd known from high school would come out of it okay. The

FBI had only just begun to target the trio of Tommy, Clay, and Jeff and had brought James in to infiltrate their little group, get some information on tape, get them caught with their hands in the cookie jar, put them away for a very, very long time.

Then, out of the blue, there was Scotlyn on Clay's phone of all places, as beautiful as he remembered. Everything about her, every memory rushed back to him, just like that. He recalled her shy smile, her wide, upturned eyes, as he told her about his dreams for the future, the way she quietly told him hers. He remembered wanting to take her hand that day he'd walked her home from school but didn't because he knew he was leaving soon.

He knew a lot of guys his age back then would've taken advantage of the situation and the obvious crush that Scotlyn had had on him, but James just hadn't wanted to do that to her. Their moments together had been brief, but her image had stayed with him, as had the feeling that she was the one, the one who'd gotten away, though he'd been the one to leave town.

It was the memory of her, of them together, that made him realize, when he thought about the things he'd done in the past, that the sometimes-life-threatening assignments he was now forced to take, that there were still good things in life, good people.

It had been in that moment, looking at her picture, that James had decided immediately, though not impulsively, that if these guys had any ill will toward Scotlyn, he'd do anything and everything to protect her, no matter what.

"Yes," James finally answered and headed out to the car.

Chapter 12

Tommy felt like he wanted to shoot Jeff. Damn kid was pacing back and forth like a tiger in a cage, just staring out the grimy windows that lined the wall of the open room in which they now all—or he and Clay, anyway—sat around in metal chairs at a table, their guns strategically placed on it to remind, though not insult, Jimmy.

Takeout containers were strewn about, betraying the fact that they were now forced to live here so they could keep watch on that girl twenty-four/seven.

Tommy looked out the window, past Jeff, and saw that it was a gray day outside. It wasn't yet two o'clock, not quite time for Jimmy to make his grand appearance, but Tommy still found himself a little nervous. He brought a cigarette to his mouth and took a drag.

Damn you, Jeff. Tommy had kicked the habit of smoking several years earlier but when Jeff had proudly displayed that girl in the chair yesterday, all Tommy could think about was where he could get some nicotine.

He was stubbing out his latest cigarette when Jeff said, almost jumping up and down, "There he is!"

Tommy looked up just as Clay was rising to his feet and saw the black Charger pulling in at a slow, easy pace.

Relaxed as always, he thought, also rising. Jimmy got easily out of the car, closed the door behind him in one motion, and began walking toward the building.

The door at the far end was open and he walked through it, past Jeff, who stared at him with both fists clenched as if he were ready, almost hoping, Jimmy would try something with him for kidnapping his girl. Jimmy made a beeline for Tommy and stopped only inches before the table, removing his sunglasses.

He took a small plastic box from his pocket that looked like one someone might keep glasses in and held it up.

"Where is she?" Jimmy asked, his eyes hard and clear.

This was a guy who was angry, but one who had his wits about him, Tommy could see. They'd have to be careful. Very careful.

"Not so fast," Tommy said, hoping Jimmy missed the slight shake in his voice.

He held out his hand for the container. Jimmy handed it over and Tommy nodded once to Clay, who patted Jimmy down while Tommy looked at the syringe, hoping he looked like he knew what he was looking for. Satisfied that this looked good enough, he handed it back to Jimmy, glancing at Clay as he did.

"He's clean," Clay confirmed.

"Very good," Tommy said. "Let's go."

He walked ahead of Jimmy while Clay and Jeff followed, just to be sure Jimmy wouldn't try anything. Tommy was still nervous, though, with Jimmy behind him. They stopped short at a room at the end of the hall. Clay and Jeff went ahead inside and Tommy pointed to the other room at the end of the hall, the one whose door locked from the outside.

"In there," he said. "I'll press this—" He gestured at a large red button on the wall. "—the door will open. You'll have five minutes. We'll be watching."

Jimmy didn't say a word, only waited. Tommy hit the button.

⁊⊙⊱

Scotlyn could hear the buzzer sound, but didn't—couldn't—lift her head toward it. She'd been trying to keep her head about her for a long time now, but had felt herself drift into unconsciousness more than a few times, and she knew she wouldn't be able to talk herself into breathing steadily much longer. She'd need her inhaler sooner than later.

"Scotlyn," a familiar voice called to her, though from a far-off distance.

She tried to focus, to push through the sleep she had fallen into, the sleep that was threatening to turn into a coma any time now.

"Hey," the voice said.

Someone gave her a couple of gentle smacks on her cheek. She groaned, trying harder. Her eyes seemed welded shut, her brain foggy. Her head felt like a loose tree branch swaying in the wind.

"Scotlyn," he said again, sharper this time, putting his hand around her neck to steady her.

She blinked, trying to focus, trying to see who was speaking her name, speaking to her in that voice that was familiar and foreign at the same time. Finally, she stilled her eyes upon him. She didn't have to blink again to know who it was.

James. He was here to save her. She didn't have to say his name for him to know that she knew. How had he known?

She half smiled at him, knowing that that didn't matter at the moment, that he was here, and that was all that mattered.

"You're here," she said.

"Yeah," he said. He took an inhaler from somewhere she didn't see and held it up to her mouth. "Here."

She inhaled once, deeply, from it, and then breathed slowly, letting the Albuterol work its magic.

"I'm going to get you out of here," he said when she focused a little more on him.

"I know," she said, slowly reaching a finger up to touch his hand that was resting on the chair's arm.

She expected him to take out a knife or something else sharp to cut the ropes, but he didn't. Instead, he reached behind him again and pulled out something she couldn't see and, still looking at her eyes, jabbed her with a needle on the side of her neck.

Scotlyn felt the sharp pinch of it and drew in a breath. "James?"

She tried to focus, but she was so tired and confused, almost in a daze, floating.

"Are you clear, now?" he asked after a couple of minutes.

"What?"

"Tell me where we went on our first date."

Why was he asking this? She blinked, trying to focus, to remember. Her head hurt, but the rest of her body was almost numb.

"Scotlyn," he snapped and her head lolled around to face him. "Our first date," he repeated.

"Uh—oh, yeah, i—it was Roman's. We danced…"

He turned, looking at the wall with the big mirror,

and nodded. He still did it in an easy, laid back way, but there was something different about his movements, something forceful and violent.

What was going on?

"James?" she asked, hoping he'd just explain. She felt too tired to ask what this was all about.

He turned back to her. "You know you can trust me, right?"

"Uh-huh." If she couldn't, she really *was* in trouble.

"Do you remember the day of the robbery last year?" he asked.

Scotlyn felt her body perk up suddenly and come to attention. Why was he bringing this up? She wanted to ask but didn't, sensing time was of an essence here, and instead nodded, trying to slow her heart and her breathing.

James looked down, turned his face slightly from the window. "Say no to these next few questions, no matter what."

What? Had she heard him right? He wanted her to *lie*?

"Do you remember the man you looked at?" he asked. "Do you remember anything about him?"

"What? James?"

He looked at her then, his eyes pleading, and she got the message. "Answer the question," he said slowly, but almost shouting.

"I—no, I don't," she said.

"Have you, in the last three months, gone to the police?"

"No," she said, shaking her head for emphasis. That was the truth.

"Other than me, have you told *anyone* of what happened that day?"

"No."

James leaned in closer, searching her eyes. His arms were on either side of the chair, but Scotlyn didn't feel protected. If anything, the way he was standing over her like that was starting to frighten her.

Suddenly, he turned toward the mirror again. "We're clear. She doesn't remember a thing."

Scotlyn continued looking at him, wondering why he was asking her this. Was he one of the robbers? A loud buzzer sounded and James took off toward the door at the other end. Wait a minute! Where was he going? He'd said he was going to get her out of here, hadn't he?

"James!" she called, but it was as if he didn't hear her. He pulled the door open forcefully and walked through it.

"James!" she cried out again, though she didn't know if he could hear her from the other side. She struggled against the ropes, feeling the raw pain from rope burns on her wrists awaken once more.

"James!" she called again because she had no idea what else to say.

But he never came back.

⌀⌀⌀

James fought past the sound of Scotlyn's voice as the door clanged shut behind him. He wanted to beat Tommy, Clay, and especially Jeff, to death and had to force his arms to stay at his sides as he said to Tommy, "Satisfied?"

"I reckon," Tommy said. "Now about that cut—"

"My fence is on the way as we speak," Jimmy said.

"Your fence?" Tommy repeated, raising an eyebrow.

Quick, James thought. "I trust him completely, just about the only person I *can* trust completely." *Pace yourself.* Slower this time, he said, "Two hundred twenty-five thousand in cash. Five o'clock tomorrow at the drop off point."

"Yup," Tommy said, the hint of a smile forming as he thought about all that money.

Keep your mind on it, Tommy, James thought. *Let it cloud everything.*

"Scotlyn for the money," James said.

"Two hundred twenty-five thousand," Tommy agreed.

"If she's hurt—" James threatened, but Tommy stopped him, laughing.

"Don't worry," he said. "Nothing will happen to your precious little girlfriend. You two can be on your way to wherever just as soon as we have our cash."

"And then it's over," James said, to which Tommy

agreed. But James knew full well that the drop off was only the beginning.

☙❧☙

Scotlyn had been in that chair seemingly for days now, save for the few times someone, looking like a certain horror movie villain in a ski mask, had hauled her to her feet and pushed her into that bathroom for five minutes at a time. Her legs and whole back ached and her arms and neck were stiff. She could only sleep for minutes at a time, until her neck would fall back in the chair and she'd instinctively snap it back into place. Mostly, she just sat and thought about things, trying to remove herself from the situation by thinking about her father, and Jane, the bookstore, what she'd draw if she drew this room. She counted the bricks in the wall several times, counted the number of times the hanging bulb above flickered. She had no idea when night or day came, or how many hours had passed. She had no idea when or if she'd be out of there.

Why had James just left her there? Why had he said he was going to get her out of there and then hadn't? What was his connection to these people? He had talked to them through that mirror like he knew them personally.

Scotlyn had looked at the mirror, at the way her hair was now matted up against her skull, at the blackened eye the last guy had given her. When he'd hauled her to her feet, he'd punched her across the face and then laughed as she'd doubled over feeling like bones had been crushed in her face. She looked at herself until she no longer saw ugliness or attractiveness in herself, until the person she saw looking back seemed like a stranger.

She looked and looked, wondering if the person on the other side was looking back, what they thought when they saw her, and what kind of person could do this to another.

She didn't know how much time had passed. It could've been days. It could've been hours. The room was starting to change colors from gray to white and back again.

Where was James?

ↄↄ

The door swung open and one of the men stepped through once again. He carried a shotgun like he always did, but instead of kneeling to untie the ropes, he took out a fancy sort of knife, flipped out the blade with a flourish, and sliced the ropes before she knew what was happening.

"All right," he said. "Your boyfriend just called. He came through for us."

Scotlyn didn't say anything, didn't want to get her hopes up or jinx anything by speaking. She tried to sit up so she could stand, but it was as if her body was welded to the chair. Her feet were numb, beyond asleep by now.

"Get up," the man said, no sympathy in his rough tone.

"I—" Scotlyn said, struggling against the numbness, trying to push up with her hands. "I can't."

He put a large hand under her arm and hauled her up on her jellified legs. She had to reach out instinctively to grab his arm so she could steady herself. She tried to keep her knees stable, but it was going to take time.

"Get a hold of yourself," he said, violently shaking her hand off his arm and pushing her forward. Scotlyn stumbled a few steps and tried to obey, but she had to cling to the wall as she walked down the dim hall with the chipped paint because she kept swaying side to side. They reached a large metal door at the end of the hall but before she could reach the handle, he said, "Stop. Turn around."

When she did, she saw he'd slung the shotgun around his back and was retrieving a blindfold from his back pocket. He put it in place over her eyes, shoved her around, and fastened it tightly. They didn't want her to know where they were, which meant they were probably close to home, still in Laurel Springs, maybe.

"All right," he said, taking her by the arm.

She stumbled along beside him, trying to keep up with his faster pace. He'd done a pretty good job with the blindfold. She couldn't see if it was night or day, could only feel pavement beneath her feet as he pulled her along.

He shoved her in the backseat of some car, told her to put her hands behind her. Scotlyn did and he put some hard plastic around them that cut into her skin. Then he pushed her down on the floorboard and her head hit someone else's booted foot, but she didn't move.

"Don't even think about getting up," he said and slammed the door.

She didn't. She thought about what he'd said earlier, how her "boyfriend" had come through for them, and wondered what exactly that meant. Was she going to see James again? He was going to have a lot of explaining to do when she did, and the first thing would be why he'd left her in that hell for who knows how long.

The man got into the front seat, said something to someone else sitting up there and the car moved forward. Scotlyn just tried to focus on breathing, and the fact that she was probably going to be free in a few minutes.

But the minutes passed by and they still drove. Scotlyn's shoulders felt like someone had injected steel right into them, and her arms were starting to feel stretched beyond their maximum length. She tried shifting in little movements, turning her neck here, moving her hands there. She guessed it was probably two hours before they stopped the car, maybe more. She could feel the car slowing and then pulling into some gravel drive, the wheels turning over it for a long time before the car came to a stop.

"Where the hell is he?" one of them asked.

"We're early," another commented. "He'll be here. He's never late."

"He'd better or we're going to have some excess baggage to unload."

Oh, no, he's talking about me. She tried not to think about what he meant when he said "unload." Shutting her eyes tight, she tried not to cry, to stay as numb as she had in that brick room.

He'll come, she told herself. *He won't leave you here like this*, though the way he'd easily left her tied to that chair made her wonder.

Please, God, she thought. *Please. I don't want to die like this.*

She could feel some tears starting in the corners of her eyes.

"There he is," one of them said, and Scotlyn's heart quickened.

She tried not to move. She could hear herself breathing and swallowed against her dry throat.

Car doors up front opened and closed. The back one did, too, but no one pulled her out of the car. She could hear them talking, though, calling to someone. A few more words were exchanged, but Scotlyn couldn't hear exactly what they were saying.

She moved her head around, straining to make out their words. Then there was a long pause before the back door opened.

"All right, sweetie," one of the men said with no

ounce of kindness in the term of endearment. "He wants to see that you're all right."

Scotlyn didn't move, just allowed the man to pull her out by the plastic around her wrists. She steadied herself on her legs.

It was chilly out now. Wind picked up, just slightly, and she could smell gravel dust. She coughed it out of her lungs. The man closest to her yanked the blindfold off, and she shut her eyes immediately against the bright gray sky.

When she was able to open her eyes again, she saw they were in an abandoned mill yard, maybe a steel mill. Buildings closer to them and far off in the distance were gutted out and hollow, and there was a fence surrounding the gravel drive they stood in.

Her eyes followed it until they landed on a black Charger several yards away. James was standing with another blond man. They were dressed in black from head to toe and both were holding shotguns.

In James's other hand was a large black bag. "What the hell did you do to her?" he called in a hard voice she'd never before heard him use.

Who *was* James?

"Hey, she's alive," the man holding her shoulder said. "That was our deal. You're lucky we didn't do more than just blacken her eye."

He said the last part with a seedy undertone, and Scotlyn knew exactly what he meant. She shivered and looked down, though she kept her eyes on James. He kept his on her.

"So?" another man asked, this one in charge, she saw, because as he stepped forward, the others stepped back a little. "Even trade? We send over the girl, you send us our money?"

There was something familiar about this guy's voice. Scotlyn searched her memory, tried to come up with something.

Who was this guy? Where had she heard his voice before?

James looked at the man with a hard gaze for a long time until he nodded once and handed the bag to the blond man without looking at him.

"He tries anything, I'll shoot her dead before you know it."

Oh, please, God, no.

James nodded once again.

The blond man had already begun walking a couple of steps when the man closest to Scotlyn pushed her forward.

"It's been nice, sweetie," he said and waved at her as she automatically turned to look at him.

She turned forward quickly and fought the urge to run. She kept her eyes on James as she passed by the blond man walking toward her captors, trying to think about him in another time, another light. His hard expression didn't change, even when she approached him. He had both hands on the shotgun, now, and when she got close, he used his body to push her along the side of the car, around the back and to the other side. When she looked back, she saw the blond man walking toward them once again. Was it over? Scotlyn's heart stilled as she started to hope, but not too much. James obviously wasn't relaxed and neither was the blond man.

"All right, take them," James said in a low voice, though not to her. For the first time, she noticed the tiny device in his ear that resembled a hearing aid. Almost the second he said the words, the man James was with, plus three other men who seemed to come out of nowhere, all drew their guns and began shouting, "Get down! Drop the bag!"

Scotlyn ducked instinctively but saw that James had not budged a muscle, that is, until Scotlyn's captors began raving incoherently, sputtering curse words, and drawing their own guns, obviously having no intentions of getting down or dropping that bag.

"Damn it!" James said all of a sudden, yanking the device out of his ear and aiming his shotgun. What happened next was a blur as he swung his leg underneath Scotlyn's to get her to fall to the ground. Her shoulder and hip hit the gravel with brutal force, sending paralyzing pain through her body. She didn't have a second to grunt in pain or curse James for doing that, as gunshots erupted all around, deafening her. She screamed, curling into the fetal position. Her captors were still cursing at James and the other men between shots. Her face pressed against the gravel, she saw one of them fall. James's shotgun kicked with force and then another fell to the ground. The last, the leader, had managed to make it around to the other side of the car. He got in and was speeding away, gravel spitting behind him. Then all of a sudden another shot sounded and the car surged forward, running straight into the fence before stopping. One of them had obviously shot the man dead.

Silence.

Scotlyn breathed hard, letting out a few cries. Suddenly, James was beside her.

"Are you hit?" he asked.

Only her eyes made a move to look at him.

"Are you hit?" he repeated in a shout.

"No!" she shouted back. "I don't think so."

She could hear the flicking of another knife and closed her eyes as he cut the plastic from her wrists. She could barely move her arms now, but managed somehow to get to on to her hands and knees before seeing the dead, motionless bodies again. Screaming and turning, she tried to run away from it all.

James's arm closed around her as he pulled her to him, one hand still holding the shotgun.

"Shhh," he said into her neck, his voice calm and kind once again. "It's over."

Scotlyn didn't want him holding her. She wanted an explanation, damn it! But she couldn't speak. She couldn't pull away, so she just leaned into him, knowing that, even though she didn't want him near her right then, she needed him, just like she always had.

Chapter 13

Scotlyn was in an almost catatonic state when the other police cars pulled into the gravel parking lot, speeding still even though the show had been over for quite some time. Big, husky officers in black uniforms all got out of the cars and immediately began surveying the scene. A woman with a red ponytail and a heavy jacket began taking pictures of the dead bodies.

One of the cops brought James and the other man over to his car and began talking with them and the other men who'd been hiding in the shadows. A big bald cop put a blanket over Scotlyn's shoulders and gave her a bottle of water. He started questioning her about the past few days and she told him everything she could remember while he jotted it all down on a notepad. He didn't ask her many questions, only when he had to, and when she was finished he told her she'd have to come down to the station and sign her statement as soon as she was ready.

A young paramedic from the ambulance treated her black eye, put some ointment on her wrists, and bandaged them up. He kept asking if she needed to go to a hospital, but she told him she didn't.

All she wanted was five minutes alone with James. That was it.

"Has anyone called my father?" she asked the big bald cop.

"I don't know. I can check for you, ma'am," he said, calling her "ma'am," even though he was obviously more than a few years older than her. He handed her a Styrofoam to-go box, which she opened to find a cheeseburger and fries. "Hope you're not a vegetarian or anything," he said, almost as an afterthought.

Scotlyn shook her head, tearing into the cheeseburger and thanking him with her mouth full. With everything that had gone on, she'd forgotten just how hungry she was, just how long it had been since she'd eaten anything. This was the best food she thought she'd ever eaten.

"Yes, ma'am, we called your father," he said, after speaking with another cop. "He was pretty worried, but we told him you're just fine. Just might be a few days before he sees you again."

"Okay," she began but then thought, *Wait a minute*—

"Days?" she repeated, shoving a fry into her mouth.

"Yup," he said, leaning one arm on his car. "These men weren't just any criminals. They were professionals, robbed places all over the southeast, and had a lot of contacts. We need you to lay low for a while until we can make sure none of those contacts come after you."

"What?" Scotlyn said, outraged. "Where? For how long?"

"We have a safe house near the beach about an hour away. Mr. McIntyre will take you there. It's important he that he disappears for a while, too."

Mr. McIntyre? Scotlyn thought, still chewing, and looked back at James, who was talking with another officer.

"He's a cop?" she asked, turning back to the bald officer.

"Not exactly," he answered, and Scotlyn just stared at him, waiting for an answer. "He was a grand larcenist for years. That boy took down so many scores—he was smooth. Took years for the FBI to catch him and when they did, they got him to work for them instead of going to jail, to help take down other crews because he knew so much. That's how we got him to help take down this crew here." The cop jutted his thumb at the three dead criminals.

Scotlyn continued looking at the cop a long time, almost waiting for him to tell her he was just kidding, but he never did, just kept his same expression until she started coughing uncontrollably, the food getting tangled inside her throat. He smacked her on the back a couple of times and handed her the bottle of water.

She took it, swallowed a gulp that seemed to stretch her throat to the point of tearing it. She could feel her eyes water as she looked back at James, trying to take in everything the cop had said about him, trying to make sense of it. James, the kind young man she'd known from high school, the one she'd fallen for, was a thief? A grand larcenist?

She shook her head, looking at the ground, trying not to walk over to James and begin hitting him, cursing him for lying to her, for playing with her emotions, and making her fall for him all over again.

He was probably planning on just leaving as soon as this was all over.

Why the hell had he come back into her life? If she'd known any of this, she'd rather he just stayed away from her. She looked over at James again, still talking with one of the cops, nodding his head. Oh yeah. They were going to talk, definitely.

When a coroner came and bagged up the bodies in big black bags, things got a little too real again and Scotlyn had to turn away. Those men, the ones who had held her hostage, were dead.

People she knew, even if she'd never seen their faces, even if they were horrible people, were dead. Scotlyn held her breath, closing her eyes to everything. She leaned forward, feeling light-headed and nauseous.

"Are you okay?" the cop asked her, and Scotlyn tried to nod, but still couldn't look up.

She couldn't look at this anymore. She wanted out of there.

Finally, some of the police officers and the coroner began to leave. James stood by his Charger, which had miraculously survived the ordeal with minimal damage, his back turned to her. Scotlyn hopped off the steps of the ambulance. The paramedic needed to get it back to the hospital anyway. But she didn't make a move to get closer to James. She just stood, watching him, knowing he was fully aware of her. She didn't know what to say, where to begin. Finally, the last of the cop cars pulled out, and it was just the two of them in that abandoned mill parking lot. She knew she was dependent on him to get her home, or to this safe house now, and he knew it, too.

It was getting dark. The sky had already turned a deep blue and a full moon was glowing overhead. Scotlyn opened her mouth a couple of times, but closed it again without saying anything. Then, suddenly, something awoke inside of her, a rage, as she remembered the lies.

She pushed the blanket from her shoulders, took two long steps toward James, and began hitting at his shoulders and arms, screaming, "You bastard! Who the hell are you?"

"Hey!" James shouted, matching the volume of her voice.

He whipped her around and picked her up with one arm by the waist. Scotlyn continued to blindly kick at him, hitting nothing but air, and shouted at him words she didn't even remember.

"Settle down!" he said forcefully, as a parent might say to a child, and that made her even angrier.

He opened the passenger side of his car and set her in, closing the door, knowing she wouldn't get out and run away because she had no idea where she was or where she could go from here.

She slumped down, folding her arms across her chest. James got in, slammed the door, started up the car, shoved it into drive, and sped out of the mill parking lot, leaving the chaos and ruin behind them. He drove with purpose. He knew where they were going.

Scotlyn looked out the window, not seeing the streetlights and eventual millhouses they sped past, refusing to look his way. All she saw was the redness of her own anger.

Chapter 14

James drove nonstop for over an hour before finally pulling off the main road and turning down a seemingly abandoned blacktop driveway. Even with the windows up Scotlyn could smell the sea spray and knew they were close to the ocean. The driveway ended in front of a small white stucco house that seemed to have windows all around. It looked like a simple white house, Scotlyn couldn't help noticing as they both got out of the car.

James led the way to the front arched doorway, knowing better than to touch, or even get near her at this point.

The door opened into a relieving coolness from the humidity around them. James hit a couple of light switches and Scotlyn walked past him, taking in the white tiled floors and white walls all around. There was hardly any furniture, only a small breakfast table with two chairs off to the side of the kitchen, a lone sofa sitting in the living room that, she supposed, showed an impressive view of the ocean though she couldn't see it for the darkness outside. James closed some curtains along the sliding glass windows and Scotlyn suddenly realized she hadn't been to the bathroom in several hours.

Not wanting to speak to him, even to ask him where the bathroom was, she walked toward an arched hallway at the far end of the room and found the bathroom just off to her left. She slammed the door behind her, letting him know how angry she still was, and flipped on the light. The bathroom was done in plain white tiles like the rest of the house, with a glassed-in shower off in the corner and clean towels stacked on a shelf right outside. After using the bathroom, Scotlyn shed her clothes, left them on the floor, and stepped into the shower. She caught a glimpse of her shoulder in the mirror and saw she had a nice black bruise on her shoulder from where she'd hit the ground hours earlier.

Well, at least it matches the one on my face, she thought, touching it slightly. She could feel her throat tightening, could feel every single memory of the past few days threatening to come back full force, to remind her that they'd really happened, but she swallowed hard, refusing to cry.

She instead focused on showering and saw that there was soap and shampoo, and thought how prepared these cops were. She hoped there was food in the kitchen. The burger had become an all-but-distant memory to her stomach. She removed the bandages from around her wrists, observing the redness around them, and stepped under the warm water.

She let it run down her body a long time before she lathered up her hair and washed it. She was just rinsing when she felt a cold chill coming from behind. She jumped and turned, seeing that James had opened the shower door but was still dressed and showed no signs of joining her.

Scotlyn screamed, covering her breasts and turning away from him, though his eyes looked at her face rather than the rest of her body.

"Get out!" she screamed.

"Scotlyn," he said calmly. "It's nothing I haven't seen before."

"Get out!" she yelled again, not knowing what else to say.

He held up his hands as if to surrender. "Just wanted to tell you I set some clothes by the sink for you, and I wanted to see if you wanted me to get you something to eat."

"You just wanted to see me naked," she countered,

turning her head, though not the rest of her body, to glare at him.

He rolled his eyes. "Whatever. The clothes are there and I'm getting Chinese."

He closed the door to the shower and then the bathroom door behind him.

Scotlyn finished up her shower and toweled off her hair and body before putting on the long-sleeved T-shirt and gray yoga pants he'd set by the sink. She wondered where the clothes had come from, but guessed the cops kept some here for when people had to make a fast break and end up here.

At least they fit for the most part, and smelled clean. She found a comb on the shelf behind the mirror and ran it through her hair a few times before emerging from the bathroom. That Chinese place must have been right around the corner because James was already setting the little white cartons on the table.

Scotlyn paused, watching him for a moment, wondering if her pride was stronger than her stomach, if she could refuse his kind gesture of getting food for her.

Her stomach rumbled, ready to feed on itself if she didn't put something in it.

She sighed. Reaching over and taking one of the containers and a plastic fork, she sat on the sofa, eating chicken fried rice and looking at the beige curtains, leaving James to eat alone.

When she was finished, she sat with her knees to her

chest, still looking at the curtains, still trying to think of a way to coherently and calmly begin the conversation she knew they had to have.

James finally came around to stand behind her, but she didn't acknowledge him. She was going to let him speak first.

"You can have the bed," he finally said, knowing he'd lost the privilege of sleeping beside her. "I'll take the couch."

He made a move to go to the bathroom, to shower, she guessed. He sounded tired, worn down, actually, and she knew the time was right.

"Not so fast," she said, still looking at the curtain.

He stopped, but said nothing.

She turned to look at him. "You owe me an explanation."

He sighed, though not heavily, not disrespectfully, and looked at the ceiling.

"Yeah," he finally said.

He walked around to the opposite end of couch and sank into it. He brought one hand up to rest the side of his face on his fist. Scotlyn looked at him a long time. He was different, she thought. There was a hardness, an intensity in his eyes now that had not been there all the time they'd spent together recently. Was this the real James? She couldn't stop looking at his eyes for a long time until she remembered he was waiting for her to ask her questions. She blinked a couple of times.

"How long were you a thief?" she began.

"Seven years."

"You started right out of high school?"

"Pretty much."

"Lie number one," she said.

"What?" he asked, grimacing.

She turned her body to face him. "You told me you worked on your uncle's ranch, did construction. That was the first lie."

James raised his eyebrows and closed his eyes for a second. "I did work on my uncle's ranch and I did do a little construction," he said, rubbing his eyes. He sighed the sigh of a man who felt he was getting just what he deserved, but hated it anyway.

"How did you get started?" she asked.

He shrugged. "After I got trampled and couldn't work anymore, I got pissed off at the world, I guess you could say, and started doing hold ups at convenience stores. Then I joined a bank-robbing crew and met a fence, a British man named Caleb, who convinced me I had what it takes to take down bigger, better scores. And I did. I took down almost two hundred in seven years—until they caught me."

He scratched the back of his head and looked her fully in the eye. He was so nonchalant about it all.

Scotlyn shook her head. She couldn't take this. She got up in a swift movement and walked to the windows, her hands rubbing her eyes.

Finally, she looked at him again and folded her arms across her chest. His expression had not changed.

"They—the FBI," she said.

"Yes."

"You work for them now?"

"Yes. However, in the criminal world, I'm still taking down scores. Guess you could say I'm a forced undercover agent."

Scotlyn's eyes darted around as she took all of this in. "How did I get caught up in this?"

James looked toward the kitchen then got up and went to it, started opening cabinets until he found a half-empty bottle of bourbon. He found a tumbler in another cabinet and poured a bit of the alcohol into it.

He leaned against the counter, drinking a little at a time, looking out the window above the kitchen sink.

Scotlyn came to stand across the island counter, waiting.

"Those three men were the ones who'd robbed that bank you had the misfortune of happening upon a few months ago," he said. "I used to work with two of them a long time ago when I was starting out. They'd been looking for you since Jeff, the one whose face you saw, let you escape. They were sure you were going to the cops, or already had, maybe, and were set to kill you."

"Oh," Scotlyn said, feeling her arms start to tremble even though the danger was now gone.

"Jeff's brutal," James agreed, then corrected himself.

"Or was, anyway." He took another drink and looked at Scotlyn. "I'm guessing that—" He pointed at her bruised face. "—is *his* doing."

Scotlyn glanced at the floor a moment before returning her eyes to James.

"Years ago, after I'd moved on to taking down crews, I lost touch with them because I moved to California, but when they started robbing bigger banks, they popped up on the Bureau's radar, and the FBI told me to make them an offer they couldn't refuse, tempt them to take down bigger scores with me, to make more money. Of course, I couldn't say no."

Scotlyn listened hard.

He took another drink before continuing. "We'd arranged what looked like a robbery at the precious metals factory to keep my cover. That's exactly what these guys wanted to get into. I met up with them and that's when I heard from Jeff that he knew some girl had seen his face, a girl they'd been hunting and had just now tracked down. They showed me a picture they'd taken of you that very morning."

Scotlyn closed her eyes, turned her head to the floor. They'd been hunting her, watching her.

"So I made a deal of my own," he said, cutting his eyes over to her.

She watched him as he took another drink.

"I told them I'd hand over half my take from the job at the metals factory if they let me work you and find out for sure that you weren't lying when you said that you didn't see a thing."

"You played me from day one."

He didn't answer. Instead, he said, "But I wasn't fast enough. Jeff got antsy, and that's when he kidnapped you. I was still undercover that day I visited you. It was all I could do not to get you out of there and take them down."

He looked down at his glass as he spoke. He was finished with his story now.

Scotlyn didn't know what to say, didn't know how to react to this. He'd protected her, but still used her to do his job. She suddenly thought about something. "What was that you shot me with the other day?"

"Saline," he answered. "They asked me to do shoot you with truth serum. As a backup. But seeing as how the FBI doesn't allow that, we faked it. It worked, too."

Scotlyn raised her eyebrows. Well, that explained that.

"I'm sorry you got caught up in this," he said, downing the rest of the drink. He set the glass in the sink and turned back around to face her with his arms crossed.

Scotlyn shook her head, still unable to make herself accept any of this. "And so, your dad…" she began.

"He knows what I do," James said. "I'm the one who convinced him to start up the garage again so it could complete the cover."

"Complete the cover," Scotlyn repeated, still shaking

her head. "He lied, too, so you could stick around and get me to fall for you and confide in you."

"Something like that."

"Damn you," she said.

He looked at her, almost fiercely, and Scotlyn felt a slight spasm.

"I fell in *love* with you," she continued nonetheless. "And you just used me to take down these criminals."

James held up a finger. "I protected you. *Protected* you."

"Oh yeah, you protected me all right, by playing with my emotions, making me think you were falling for me just to get some confession out of me."

She was really raging now, though the words were clear. James started to say something else, but she cut him off with, "How could you lie about your feelings for me? How could you play me like that?"

Her heart was racing, her face on fire.

"I did *not* play you," he said. "Yes, you were a victim who, unfortunately, got caught up in this, but I didn't just make that deal just to save some random person's life."

"The hell you didn't," she said, backing away, refusing to believe anything he told her now. She was shaking. "How many other lies were there? Did your mother really die or was that just another lie to 'relate' to me and get me to trust you?"

She knew how cruel that last question was and could

see from his frozen expression that he had been telling her the truth, at least about that.

She stopped and blinked a couple of times before looking at the floor.

"I didn't lie to you, Scotlyn," he said, finally, coming around the counter to close the distance between them.

She backed farther away. "Get away," she seethed, struggling against the steel trap that was enclosing her lungs.

He stopped walking but did not stop talking. "I do love you."

"No!" she said, turning away now and doubling over. She couldn't breathe. "You don't. I—I don't even *know* you. S—stay away—stay away from me."

"Scotlyn," he said again. "Are you all right?"

"What do you care?"

She finally reached the wall and slid down it, her hands over her ears, eyes closed. She couldn't see anything, couldn't hear anything.

James was at suddenly her side. She tried to push him away, but could only manage to hold up her hand. That's when he put an inhaler in front of her.

"Here," he said. She looked at the beige wall. "Scotlyn!" he said. "Breathe, please."

She had to give in. The steel trap was too strong for her to fight alone. She took a deep breath from the inhaler and waited. She didn't thank James, didn't say a thing to him, but as she finally, mercifully filled her lungs with a sweet, deep breath, she allowed herself to look into his dark green eyes, just as he looked into hers.

Chapter 15

The next day, Scotlyn stood with her arms crossed, staring at the beach just beyond the deck. The gray waves pushed in gently, pulled out again, making soft roars as they did, over and over. It was hypnotizing. It was almost sunset and was getting cold. She could feel the chill beginning to lie on her skin.

She never acknowledged James each time he came out to stand beside her, even when he looked at her a long time, even when he offered to get her dinner. She didn't know if she was just too withdrawn, in shock, or too angry to even look at him.

Whatever the case, she didn't respond, even now as

he stood a few steps away from her, leaning his back against the railing.

He didn't look at her this time. "I meant what I said," he said finally.

The waves crashed, reaching farther inward. A seagull called overhead.

"When it comes to how I feel about you."

Scotlyn blinked against the wind in her eyes.

"I hate my life," he continued, still looking at the house rather than at her. "Same danger, over and over. It's like it's never going to end—I hate it." He paused for a minute, taking his time. "But I think I could handle it if you were with me."

Scotlyn could feel her body still even more than it already was.

"If you feel like you could forgive me, stay with me."

Scotlyn looked at the sand, soft and white and sprinkled with grass, below the deck.

"Because I love you. I probably always did."

The deck railing was splintered and cracked, Scotlyn noticed.

"When I came back, when I saw you again, everything seemed...I don't know, not as bad. I was actually happy for the first time in a long time. The dangerous part of my life didn't matter so much anymore because you were with me."

Scotlyn closed her eyes. She had been happy for the

first time in a long time, too, and knew that was why she was so angry and in shock right now. She'd known all along that she'd always loved James and, even now, she always would.

She was angry with herself, angry because she couldn't just turn away from him, but she wasn't directly angry with him, she realized for the first time. Maybe it was because, despite the lies, she knew he was telling the truth now, and maybe it was because she knew the lies had protected her, kept her alive.

For the first time in hours, she turned to look at him. He was standing with his hands in his pockets, looking away, but when she looked at him, he turned his head in her direction, though still he looked down, not pushing her. Could she forgive him? A part of her, the bigger part that understood why he'd lied already had forgiven him, but another part kept telling her to stay where she was, to never forgive and never forget.

Scotlyn shook her head. *Oh, damn it all to hell*. She uncrossed her arms, reached out slowly, and grabbed at his sleeve, feeling the stiffness, the cold, the dryness in her hands.

She was so cold, she suddenly realized. She tugged on him, bringing them closer together, until she was able to put her arms around him. It was only then that he returned the gesture, the warmth from his body colliding with the chill of hers. She pressed the side of her face against his and hit at his side a couple of times before grabbing the hair at the back of his head and kissing him with a violence she didn't know she had in her.

Their lovemaking was different this time, desperate, severe, as if they'd just grabbed onto one another and held on, as tight as they could, as if the other would disappear if they didn't.

When it was over, they stared at one another a long time, never saying a word until they both fell into a long, deep sleep.

Scotlyn didn't know what time it was when she woke, but the bright sun was shining through the windows that went along two walls. She stretched, her body stiff from the night before. James wasn't there, but she heard the shower running, so she didn't worry. She reached on the floor and grabbed his shirt, tossing it over her body as she went to the kitchen to make coffee. She hoped there was coffee.

She found some in the fridge, though she didn't know how old it was. She put some in the filter, filled the water container, and stood over the pot, watching as it brewed until she heard James coming up behind her. She turned.

He wore jeans and was running a towel roughly over his still-wet hair.

"Morning," he said, tossing the towel on the counter.

"Hey," she said and realized that was the first time she'd spoken to him in nearly twenty-four hours, though they hadn't left one another. The coffee pot spewed and hissed behind her. They looked at one another a long time, but neither made a move to get closer to the other, despite last night.

Scotlyn knew what he wanted to say, or ask, and she knew they needed to talk. She took in a deep breath and looked out the window.

"It's going to rain," he observed, looking across the hollow living area, at the now gray sky beyond the floor-to-ceiling sliding glass window.

The coffee pot finished up, but suddenly, Scotlyn didn't want any.

"Did you know how much I liked you in high school?" she asked.

He glanced at her, then shrugged, and shook his head, looking all around the room.

"Then when you left," she said. "I never really stopped thinking about you. I dated, yeah, of course, but it was like you were always the one in the back of my mind. I fell in love with the idea of you. Then, you came back."

His eyes moved to the floor then back to her.

"I wasn't sure if it was you at first," she said. "I'd thought about you so much that, when I did finally see you, it was like it wasn't real."

"But it was," he said.

"Yes, it was. Then the more time we spent together, I realized I was in love with more than just an idea. I *am* in love with you, even now, after…"

He waited, knowing this wasn't the end of it.

"I just don't know if that's enough to get past—I don't know. The life you led, the one you live now—"

"You wouldn't be put in any sort of danger, ever. I'd see to that."

Scotlyn shook her head. No, that wasn't her concern. James saying that to her made her realize something all at once. "It's not that," she continued, focusing on the floor. "If anything ever happened to you—"

"A few more years, I'll be done. I will have served my time."

"And then?"

"Then?"

"Yes, then. What will the reformed thief do, then, after he has served his time? Will he go back to his old ways?"

"No," he said, never batting an eye, never changing his blank expression. "He's got over a million in accounts in the Caymans—good money. He'll move to the south of Florida, take it easy, take care of his girl, and set up her father with some good doctors."

"How do I know it's going to end like that? What happened a couple of days ago—"

"Proves that I can take care of myself, and you."

Scotlyn shook her head, turned away, her eyes

closed. Damn, how she wanted to believe him. "Is it always that bad?"

"No, not always."

"How often? I mean, what are the odds that in these next few years, or weeks, you'll see that again?"

She looked at him, searching his eyes though she knew he could lie to her easily and get away with it.

"It's rare."

"I'd like a number," she said. "So I'll know what I'm dealing with."

"Can't give you that. All I can give you is here and now and the fact that I love you and—"

"And the promise that *maybe* we'll live 'happily ever after'?"

"That's all I can give you, baby. For a few years, I'm going to still be immersed in all these dangers, with all these criminals. You can't deal with that, you should walk right now."

Scotlyn ran her hands through her hair and pulled at it, frustrated and confused. She needed to get away, to run hard and fast until she couldn't think anymore. She pushed her body away from the counter and started walking toward the deck. Despite the chill, she went clear out to the beach. The waves were softer this morning, quieter. The sky had blackened even more and thunder was starting to rumble overhead.

"Come back in," he said, his tone even and calm.

She turned to face him, seeing he'd thrown a T-shirt

on now. "I waited for you," she said. A few raindrops started to fall around them, hitting them on their faces here and there. The wind picked up. "Fourteen years. Somehow I knew you were going to come back. That's the only reason I can think of as to why I never got married, never really fell in love with anyone. I was waiting on *you* the whole time."

He didn't respond, only looked at her. What could she say? How could she do it again?

"I never knew where you were or what you were doing," she said. "But somehow, I knew you were coming back."

She walked closer to him, until their bodies were just inches apart. The rain was starting to fall harder around them.

"*Will* you come back to me again? Will you tell me that I'm not going to waste my life waiting?"

He took a second before answering. "I will."

Scotlyn could feel a sudden release in her shoulders and started crying. She didn't know what she was doing in the long run. All she knew was what she wanted here and now.

"Damn you," she said. "I wish I didn't love you."

⟲⟳⟲

James gently woke her from her steady slumber with a hand on the side of her face. He pointed to a cup of coffee on the nightstand and then told her it was almost time to go if she wanted to shower first. The darkness under his eyes betrayed that he'd obviously been up for a while.

Scotlyn stretched and looked at the plastic alarm clock on the bedside table. Almost ten. She'd spent ten hours in a deep, dreamless sleep. She sat up and took a sip of the coffee James had set out for her, noting how perfectly he'd fixed it, with just the right amount of cream and sugar, knowing for a while now how she took it. She kissed him quickly, almost without looking at him, before getting out of bed and going to the bathroom to shower.

She scrubbed herself furiously in the shower, knowing the decision that was on her shoulders, knowing she had to let James know something before they parted ways that day. He'd made it clear what he wanted yesterday morning, though the rest of the day yesterday they'd barely mentioned it at all.

Mainly, Scotlyn had given in to her curiosity about his past, questioning him about his first score, the people he'd worked with—surprised to find out how tight they were, like family. She asked him what his life had been like, his days, how he'd prepared for jobs and found out about them, how he'd finally gotten caught. She questioned him as if she was doing a research project on reformed thieves until she felt guilty for prying so much, even though he answered all of her questions thoroughly and patiently. It was surreal, yet comforting in a strange way, hearing him talk about this. Despite those hours on the couch, talking nonstop with James, resting her feet in his lap, it had seemed like a quiet day.

She'd thought and thought, even through their conversations, knowing exactly what she wanted to do. But she's never said it because the sensible voice in her head kept telling her that if she did this, if she agreed to wait for James, she'd most likely be begging life for a broken heart because she knew deep down how dangerous his job, his life, was. He'd even admitted it! *'Same danger, over and over.'*

Scotlyn replayed those words in her mind as she studied herself in the mirror now, running her fingers through her wet hair, noting that the bruise on her face was already fading.

What good could possibly come from this?

Scotlyn looked at herself a moment longer before turning and padding barefoot back to the bedroom. James wasn't in there, but had set her clothes, which he'd washed and dried, on the bed for her. Her Celtic cross—her mother's Celtic cross—was beside her shirt. Scotlyn dressed quickly and picked it up, studying it. It was simple, but beautiful, with just a few ornate carvings in the metal.

Scotlyn ran her fingers over it. She wore it almost every day. It belonged to a person she couldn't remember, a person who had left her without looking back, and still, she wore it. Scotlyn fastened it around her neck, took one last look around the room, and went to the living room where she found James leaning against the kitchen counter, fiddling with the knobs on a small silver radio, switching from station to station. Funny, Scotlyn hadn't even noticed it before now.

"Looking for something in particular?" she asked, leaning against the doorframe, trying to forget that this might be the last time she saw the love of her life.

James shrugged, though he didn't look at her. He finally stopped when he came across a Bruce Springsteen song and turned it up a little, letting the sound reverberate throughout the room. Scotlyn recognized it right away. It was one of her favorites, a slower, yet steady and rhythmical one she remembered listening to over and over in high school.

She hummed along with the song until James came over to her and held out one hand.

"You dance?" he asked, a half-smile on his face, echoing their first date at Roman's.

"Here?" she asked, uncrossing her arms and straightening her back.

"Why not?"

She raised her eyebrows and looked around the room once. Well, there certainly was enough space with the lack of furniture, and yeah, she wanted to dance with him. She put her hand in his and let him pull her to him. She put her arm around his shoulder and gently pressed her forehead to his neck, her movements instant and without hesitation or nervousness this time. He rested one arm at her waist and held her other hand with his as they swayed slowly with the music. He didn't turn her this time, just kept her close as they let the music move throughout their bodies. When it was over, another song started up almost immediately, but James stopped moving, stopping Scotlyn with him. She tilted her head to look at those dark eyes. He just looked back into hers for a long while before finally taking her chin in his hand and smiling the smallest of smiles.

Scotlyn smiled back at him just as he pulled his body from hers to walk across the room and turn off the radio.

"You ready?" he asked when he turned back, and she nodded.

He hit the lights on the way out, letting her go out first.

Always the gentleman, she couldn't help thinking, remembering how he'd moved her to the inward part of the sidewalk on their first date. Suddenly, the full memory of that day came back to her, and her chest began to hurt. After James locked up and fell into step beside her, she took his hand, holding it until they reached the car.

 လာ

Hours later, James sped the Charger along the

highway, weaving in and out of cars, never taking his eyes from the road. Scotlyn stole glances at him now and then, wanting to freeze his profile in her mind. Despite still not knowing her decision at the safe house earlier, she knew now what she was going to say. How could she begin to wait on him again, never knowing this time not only when or if she'd see him again, but if he'd live through those next few years to come back to her? It wouldn't be a life she'd want to live, not knowing from one moment to the next whether or not he was dead or if his life was in danger.

She closed her eyes. She'd be better off if she cut loose of him right now, while she could still move on, find someone new and settle down, or just live her life day to day and forget about James. That was what she needed to do, and she knew it.

Scotlyn's heartbeat picked up as James pulled the Charger into her driveway slowly and put it in park. She didn't make a move right away to get out of the car, trying to coherently formulate the answer she knew she had to give, glad that the police told her father that she'd call him when she returned home, that he wasn't there, waiting on her.

She needed just this last minute with James before reality came back full force. They sat for a long time, still not looking at one another, waiting as Scotlyn gathered her thoughts. Finally, she took a breath and pushed her hair behind her ear. "Um—" she began.

James was quiet.

She reached around the back of her neck and unfastened the Celtic cross. "This belonged to my mother," she said. "She wore this all the time, and left it behind when she took off. I wear it almost every day, though I don't really know why."

James turned his eyes to look at the necklace in her hand. Scotlyn took his right hand and dropped the necklace in it.

"This means a lot to me. You'd better not lose it," she said. "Because I expect you to give it back when you come back to me."

He looked at her then. His expression didn't change, though she could see something flickering in his dark eyes. Scotlyn smiled at him and nodded.

"I promise I will," he said.

"I'm going to hold you to that," she said, and at that moment, they both leaned in until their lips met in a kiss.

About the Author

Tanya W. Newman was born and raised in Upstate South Carolina, where she discovered her love of a good story, and where she decided to try to write a book of her own at the age of ten. When she was finished, the story was a whopping thirty pages, but nonetheless cemented her love of writing and storytelling, a love that led to a Bachelor of Arts in English from University of South Carolina Upstate, and a Master of Arts in English from Clemson University. She has continued through her work as a college instructor and Library Specialist.

Now married to her wonderful husband, Mark, for ten years, Newman still resides in Upstate South Carolina, where she sets many of her stories. When not indulging in writing or reading, she enjoys a good cup of coffee; watching movies (usually an action/adventure with a love story added in) or reruns of *The Golden Girls*; going for long walks; and spending time playing with, snuggling, and reading to her adorable son and daughter.

http://awritingmom.blogspot.com

www.ingramcontent.com/pod-product-compliance
Lightning Source LLC
Chambersburg PA
CBHW071153170626
46809CB00002B/879